Of The First Magnitude

~I~

I0535966

~Volume 1~

Facing Revelation

An Emerging

~Volume 2~

iRise

An Algorhythm of Freedom

~Volume 3~

Quantum Engineering

Introspecting the Rabbit Hole

~Volume 4~

Algorhythmic Insight

Poetic Analysis of the Journey

Copyright Notice:

Read it!

Integrate it!

Live it!

Truth, that is...

© 2018 – Michael J.M. Phoenix - All Rights Reserved.

Emergent Strategies LLC
PO Box 245
Winona, MO. 65588
https://3m3r3g.com
orders@3m3rg3.com

Ordering Information:

ISBN: 978-1-7337454-0-6

Quantity sales. Special discounts are available on quantity purchases by corporations, associations, and others. For details, contact the publisher at the address above.

Cover Art: Sam Whelan - https://www.samwhelan.net/

~ Volume 1 ~

Facing Revelation

An Emerging

By Michael Phoenix

Due to the graphic nature of this book, reader discretion is advised. Not suitable for a young audience.

Table of Contents

Chapter 1 – Dreaming of Charlie

"Hey Deebo, you gonna pass the blunt," I said as Jeremy pulled for the fifth time on the sacred herb wrapped in a Philly. "Chill dawg, smoke on this." Wallace handed back another blunt freshly lit as smoke curled upward off the tip.

"Yea..chh," Jeremy said as he began choking, trying to hold the smoke in while talking. "Cuz we bout to take flight…ckhfhh"

"I don't care how many blunts we're rollin', you betta' pass that blunt," Lavont emphasized, as he put his hand up in a pimp-smack gesture to Jeremy.

"Damn dawg, you rollin another blunt. How many you rollin," I asked Wallace as he put the blunt to his lips. Wallace held up a bag full of the high grade weed after it had been processed through a homemade vaporizer made of a plastic bag, a glass bowl, and a heat gun.

Six blunts later, the car was filled with dense smoke, and five very high individuals. "Don't forget we got practice tomorrow," Lavont said as he opened the door. "You better not be late either. Ain't no color'd people time 'round here just cuz you got high the nigh' be'fo," smoke continuing to billow out as he talked.

In a haze of moments passing by, with no coherent connection from one to the next, I found myself lying sprawled, face first, on my make-shift King sized bed of two dormitory twin-beds pushed together.

"Greetings," a voice echoed somewhere in my consciousness. I reached with all my ability to stop my reality from spinning. Floating through moments, as if I were somehow disconnected from my body, but yet, feeling on the verge of splitting out through my head. I could feel my mind turning in on itself in an effort to locate the source of the voice. My head began to ache as I increased the effort of turning my mind to find the voice.

"You won't find me while you strain as you do," the voice said. "You must relax your mind and open your heart if you wish to find me."

I took a deep breath, unsure if I was dreaming, or hallucinating, or both. As soon as the exhale began, I knew I was dreaming, yet entirely lucid. My awareness drifted out through the back of my body and I hovered looking at myself looking into darkness. I rotated my awareness only to meet two cat like eyes. Again, words began forming in my mind that were not my own. A moment later, I knew these thoughts were of the cat, but its mouth was not moving.

"I noticed you're aware of these words. You who's making the decision to read this book.

"You may call me Charlie, I am Michael's dead cat."

Why are you talking to me as if I'm reading a book, and you're not dead, you're at mom and dad's house, still quite alive.

"I'm not speaking to you Michael, and this is not a time period of the present day. You are piercing the veil of time and are witnessing something that is yet to come in your linear perception of time.

"And no, you're not crazy. Animals do actually communicate to people. So you can do what you do to dissolve that mental construct from your mind, Michael. Fear not though, most humans are still too dense to actually perceive the communication.

If you're not talking to me, then who are you talking to?

"As I said, to the one reading this book, a book you have yet to compose, Michael." *I have no desire to write a book, so you can get on with that Chuck.* "Very well.

"Now that you have seen the peculiar nature of Michael's predisposition to taking things personally, let's take a moment to get acquainted with the cosmic pattern known as Mike Morris."

What are you talking about?

"Silence will benefit you presently, Michael. All will become clear in due time. It will be your challenge to remain calm in the midst of your inner storm."

A moment later, I was at my old high school. The bell had just rung and students were making their way out of the door. *Hey that's me, what are we doing.*

"As I said Michael, you will need to simply observe what transpires here. Your questions are not needed. Now please, if you would, embrace silence."

The me of my memory began making his way down the sidewalk. Next to him his best friend. A few feet back, a girl in their class.

Oh shit, I know what this is. "Silence. Observe."

"I bet you wish your brother was still here," the girl said.

Rage flushed through Michael as he observed the flashback. *What, why I do I feel that?* "You better shut the fuck up," Mike said. "Before I curb stomp your ass you stupid fuckin cunt."

I watched as my old self uttered those words to a harmless 17 year old girl. A brief moment later, my best friend grabbed me around my ribs and pushed me away towards lunch. The girl turned back towards school crying.

Oh fuck, I actually did that. That rage wasn't me in the now, that was the rage of then, what the fuck was I so mad about?

Before I knew it I was back in the shapeless void of my awareness, staring at the golden cat eyes. "Why did you show me that, Chuck?"

"I didn't show *you* that, I revealed it to the one reading this book. As you have yet to realize Michael, not everything is about you."

So what're you trying to accomplish?

"I have already told you, I am revealing your back story."

You sure got a funny way about doin it.

"Your opinion is inconsequential to the purpose of this book."

What is the purpose of this book, then?

"As I have said, to reveal your back story. Now, no more questions from you Michael. Please make it a point to simply observe what transpires."

Make it a point to Chuck You Farlie..

"Precisely why it will be your challenge to remain calm in the midst of your inner storm. Do you think you can call forth the ability to do this, Michael."

A tightness began to form in my chest, as heat flushed through my neck and face. Fists clinched, I said nothing.

"That is a start. Thank you for making this effort, Michael. As for you reading, this book acts as a relational node in the matrix of your experience; a certain type of relationship has formed. As you light these words with your awareness, it will be your responsibility to hold the space for the mental and emotional resonances to arise, be present, and pass through. In this process, you will be allowing yourself to witness transformation, and thereby, cultivating an opportunity for such in your own experience, if you so desire. Now, back to the exposition."

A flash of light burst through my mind's eye, and as the glare began to fade, I was in the back seat of my high school superintendent's car looking at my past self in the passenger seat, and the superintendent in the driver's seat. A superintendent who was also my parish priest. It was a few weeks before the beginning of my senior year.

"Michael," he said, "I have a few questions to ask you. This is not an easy conversation, but I have to ask. Over the summer, there was a condom found in..." whatever he said next was lost in unconsciousness as my awareness immediately shifted to the giant knot now in my stomach. *You guilty son of bitch you... goin off and havin sex in your coach's office... but you got caught.* My mind drifted back to that night. A night when all the dreams of a virgin boy came true, yet, in one drop of the booty, shattered dreams of a senior starting quarterback were the result. No longer was the only guilt I was feeling belonging to the past-self sitting in the passenger seat, but also to my present-self for... "Michael, did you hear my question," he said.

"Yes, Father, I had sex with her that night." Immediately the fabled words of my older brother shot through my mind, *you could have denied it, they couldn't prove anything.* And instantly, the rebuttal, *but that's not me.*

"Now I've talked to the school board," Father went on, "and we've decided that in order to continue going to school here, there are some things you need to agree to."

"Such as."

"Well, first, you'll have to not play the first two football games of the season. Second, you'll have to do 150 hours of community service. And third, go to anger management counseling."

"Wait, what the fuck does having sex have to do with playing football. You do realize that I'm trying to get a scholarship to play football in college right?"

"I know this Mike, and you know how I feel about football, it's the last thing I want to keep you from doing. But given everything over this last year, we feel we have to look out for what's best for our school."

I saw my past-self turn towards the window and stare off into space, considering the implications of this latest revelation.

Guilt continued to linger in my own emotions as I pondered back to that fateful day. A day that entirely changed my outlook on life.

Football had been the only thing to keep my sanity in check. My entire life revolved around football season, and it had since as far back as I could remember. Being the youngest of six boys, all of which who played football. Five of us that went on to play in college. And all of which set great stock in football season, missing two games of my senior year because I had sex was nothing less than a life altering event. Sex in no way compared in value to football. Sex to me, at that point in my life, was a fleeting and over dramatized past time.

Football was life!

The guilt from that day still haunted many of my dreams. Countless times I've dreamt being in a locker room getting ready for a game, only to see that I've missed the game entirely as everyone else is getting undressed after having lost.

From that point forward, football became less of a focal point in my life, to be replaced with… well, nothing. As I sat in the back seat reflecting on my past self who was reflecting on his future, a tornado of emotions ripped through my gut. Slowly the scene began fading into silvery wisps of mist until I found myself facing those same two cat eyes.

"So it seems you have yet to fully recognize a valuable truth from this lesson, Michael."

Hey fuck you, I thought this book wasn't about me. Why don't you get on with your back story.

"Ah, but you see, it is about you."

"Fuck off. Just finish this shit so you can leave me the fuck alone."

"In time. All will be revealed in time. In as much as this part of this book is for the readers to gain a deeper sense of your character, this too is an opportunity for you to resolve much that has been left buried in your psyche. It is no secret that you have skeleton's hidden in your past. Your brothers even now worry about you. Some of them more so than others. And with good reason. Why do you think your oldest brother came for you that night you were alone while most the rest of them were at his house watching football? Why did he pound on the door as he did? Why did he not give you an option to come or not? Why did he tell you that you were coming to his house, not as a request, but as a statement of fact?

"Do not think for a moment, Michael, that you have hidden your shadows such that others cannot see them. Your shadows are on display for those who are perceptive enough to see them. Do not underestimate those closest to you."

Before I could speak, I was sucked through a high speed replay of some distinct moments of decision in my life. Watching my 7th-grade-self take a condom out of the trash, a condom my 7th-grade-self had placed in my classmate's locker only an hour before. Unrolled and hung from his coat hook. I watched as I, for a second time, put it back in his locker on the same coat hook.

A moment later, I'm in my principal's office watching my 7th-grade-self admit to doing it. *Why in the fuck did you always admit to that shit? Why did you never lie about it?*

13

Bringing my awareness back to the slideshow of my life, I saw I was now sitting in my pastor's lounge one Saturday after church service a few weeks before my sophomore year. I watched my younger self ponder with anxiety why, in his sermon, Father had mentioned prayers for the family of my classmate. The very same classmate who I had put the condom in the locker in 7th grade.

"What happened Father? What were you talking about in your sermon?"

"This is not easy Mike, but your friend, your classmate committed suicide. He shot himself with a gun."

The look of dread on my younger self's face said it all. I watched as he came to the full recognition of the situation. I watched as he relived the pain of his cousin's suicide only 5 years previous. Even now as I sat watching myself, a taste began to salivate through my mouth. A taste that I had long since associated with death. It was a wretched taste that only came when something close to me died. A taste that I had no control over removing from my mouth. A taste for which the timing of its arrival was in no way under my direct control.

Moments later, I witnessed countless moments pass, of daily stating my prayer request for my classmate's soul during theology class that sophomore year. I watched as my depressed younger self would find his only respite from the tragedy that was his life in the form of a football, and a football field. Then a basketball and a basketball hoop. Then spikes, and a track, and hurdles. Then restart the cycle with summer conditioning. Nothing else mattered. Athletics was the entire purpose of life. I watched my younger-self swim through a sea of memories with a singular focus of getting a football scholarship.

Suddenly, the swimming slowed as a scene arrived towards the end of my senior year. My track coach confronting me, asking me why I didn't go to the Conference track meet.

My response, "I went to a religious retreat with Father Green, and a few friends."

"Well, unfortunately, since you didn't go to the Conference meet, you can't go to Districts, and consequently, State."

"Are you serious? You're not going to let me go to the District meet because I missed Conference for going to a religious retreat. This is a Catholic school right? And you do know I have one of the fastest times in state in the 110's, right?"

"Well, they use the times you get at Conference to set you up at District."

"Whatever, this is bullshit, I'm done. I won't be at any more track meets. I'm gonna get ready for football next season." *This is all because her dad is the head track coach, and he's pissed I fucked her and she got in trouble too...fuck him.*

I watched as my younger self turned and walked out the front doors of the school he had gone to his entire school career from preschool through his Senior year. I watched him walk, carrying the resentment of feeling the hypocrisy of an organized religion who preaches forgiveness, and does little in the way of enacting it. Never again would he consider himself a Catholic. Forever had his faith in such a religion been shattered.

As I sat watching, I realized that it was this particular situation, of quitting track that was the cracking of the seed of realization. Quitting track that year was the only thing I have ever quit for no justifiable reason. I liked running track, it was something I enjoyed. And there was no reason to not run other than someone else saying I was not allowed. This reason, in itself, does not justify quitting doing something I love. And yet, as I watched my younger self walk through those doors, the residual feeling was one of understanding. Of clarity. At that time, it was a shimmer of something that had yet to find its way into my conscious mind. But at that moment, it was a sliver in my mind that began to act as a wedge, separating what other's gave me to be the truth, and what I, in my own being, have come to know to be true.

"So you see, Michael, the value of self-reflection, of introspection," Charlie asked the rhetorical question as my mind's eye filled with the blackness of a void.

"If you mean the fact that I feel things I haven't let myself feel in many years, yes. But if you mean to point out to me all the ways I'm fucked up, I'd appreciate you just keeping silent."

Eyes opened four feet in front of my face. "Michael, remember, self-reflection is not something anybody else does to you. If you are shown the error of your ways, what you choose to respond with is entirely your own decision. You taking the implication that I may be poking at your flaws is a tendency that will pave your way to much pain and needless suffering if you're not careful."

"Anyway, I thought you weren't talking to me. I thought you were talking to the readers," I said, disdain dripping on every word.

"I am, and I did. You see that book at your feet?" I looked down to see a book with a black cover, with a title loosely drawn on it. "I encourage you to pick it up," he said, casually preening his ghost-like paw.

I reached for the book. As my finger touched it, an energy shot up my finger, into my arm and down through my body to my feet. "That book," Charlie said, "represents a possibility of something that may change the way you see things. You might consider reading it."

I looked at the book. Looked back to Charlie. He sat, staring me in the eyes. A blaze of heat ignited in my chest. I looked back at the book and began flipping through the pages.

Chapter 2 - Class

"This is real," I uttered unconsciously lurching forward to a sitting position. Awakened from my sleep, my mind was reeling from the dream I just had. Trying to grasp at any semblance of sanity I could, *that was the craziest dream I've ever had,* was all I could think. The craziest part is that the dream felt more real than the reality of me being awake.

So what the fuck is that book supposed to mean? And why did my dream feel more real than what I know as reality? I thought to myself.

"This is too fucked up," I said, voicing my frustration.

I need to stop smoking so much fuckin weed, I thought as I nodded my head in agreement with myself.

Getting up at 5:30 in the morning for winter conditioning wasn't exactly what I most wanted to be doing, I'd rather have my ass in a warm comfortable bed debating whether or not I wanted to go to class that day, or stay in and get blazed. On top of it all, I wake up from a crazy dream seven minutes before my alarm is supposed to go off.

Pissed off I missed seven minutes of precious sleep, I roll out of bed. Mind-fucked over the dream, I go to the mirror trying to gain that semblance of sanity. And taking one look at myself, I laugh at my own confusion. It's all I can do, I mean shit, my mind is blown both philosophically and chemically, and now I'm pissed I missed seven minutes of glorious sleep. Gone, never again can I get that seven minutes back, all because of a stupid ass dream.

Hey, at least I got Filler's class today, I get to meditate…or sleep… yeah, probably sleep.

I always love going to a class that actually stimulates my mind, instead of some monotone joke of a professor thinking he actually has something to teach me that I don't already know. To be honest, it gets fucking pathetic sometimes when I think about paying thousands of dollars to learn something I could get in a book from the library, or twenty minutes on the internet.

But not Filler's class, his class was always stimulation for my mind. It actually gave me fertilizer to ponder and digest.

As I walked into class after my morning routine of weights and food, my mind was busy sorting through the guests I invited to my pity party in celebration of my thinking that I should be in bed. Being too tired to care about trying to finish the half-ass homework I did the night previous, and wondering if Elyssa would sit next to me today, I sat in the chair closest to where I found myself at the moment.

It had been junior high since I had a groin-fire, stomach churning, heart throbbing crush on someone, and now here she was, *Why don't you quit being a pussy about it and do something, ya pussy…you're never gonna get anywhere if you keep bein a pussy…ya pussy,* that inner voice reminiscent of my older brother just seemed to pop up telling me what to do.

"Hey what up Lavont?"

"Chillin bro, tired as fuck though," slouching in his chair, looking like he was getting ready to take a nap.

"No shit, fuckin runnin and shit is some bullshit at six in the morning." I said, following Lavont's cue that it was nap time. "Well, maybe not complete bullshit if you wanna actually be good." It amazed me when I first met him; I couldn't help but wonder how this inner-city black guy from Dade county became like a brother to a white farm-boy from Nebraska. I was always fed the impression that inner-city black guys were worthless, and nothing but gun-toting trouble. Yet, here I was talking to an intelligent human being simply looking to better himself as any worth-while person should.

Now don't get me wrong, he certainly played the part well. Looking like a thug, being 6'3, 220 pounds of solid muscle with countless tattoos, dreadlocks and with a walk that says "I don't give a fuck." To judge this book by its cover though, is to miss out on a person who actually gives a damn about not only himself, but everyone he cares about.

Guess it's that true type of friendship, the type of relationship that lasts through all the bullshit to see better days. Brotherhood is a good word for it.

By this time, professor Filler was already well into his normal far-out epilogue about consciousness and transcendence of the ego. Today, though, he was carrying on about our eternal self, and as he continued my mind just kind of, seized the moment, literally. As if there were a hundred different thoughts running through my head without any particular attention to any of it. Then, out of nowhere, he said something and my brain reached an arm out through my forehead and grabbed the words as they were pouring out of his mouth.

In that moment, all other thoughts ceased and my attention was squarely focused on devouring everything he was saying. As he drew a giant circle from the top of the marker board to the bottom, he was saying, "now imagine this is everything that you are, your entire being, everything that composes you is represented by this circle."

As he said this, I started to feel the hollowness in my chest defrost, and this unexplainable warmth began to seep into my heart. At that moment, I knew he was saying something of significance for me.

Turning back to the board, he put an arrow on the left and right sides of the circle, "and these arrows represent that you reach out into eternity, signifying that you are never ending, eternal and infinite. Reaching beyond time itself."

Then out of nowhere, a voice of doubt arose in my mind, *This is bullshit, what the fuck is this guy talking about, don't tell me you actually believe this shit, you're an atheist, you don't believe this completely invalid conjecture.*

Responding to that voice in my head, *Nah now, wait just a second, if I...If I just outright deny everything he's sayin I'm not bein fully accountable to the pursuit of knowledge you and I are both passionate about. Sure I can counter everything he's sayin by empirical rationale, but what if he leads us to an understanding about my self that wouldn't be possible otherwise. All I'm sayin is just hear him out.*

By now my mind was obviously beginning to question what I was hearing. This was starting to sound like the bullshit that I heard back in high school during one of the thousands of theology classes I had to suffer through on a daily basis, "you have soul and Jesus is your savior because he's both human and divine, and you'll have eternal life through him."

Frankly, in my eyes, the validity of spirituality, and specifically, religious conjecture, carried about as much weight in an argument as a pedophile priest. *Go Fuck Yourself!* basically summed up how I felt about someone trying to convince me about an afterlife.

Today, though, it was different as I heard Filler saying what he said. In all my time being Catholic, there was only one instance that I could say I actually felt anything that remotely felt like the love talked about in the gospel. The other umpteen years it felt like a job, something I had to do because I was under the pressure and impression that if I didn't, well, eternity in hell. That's not a pretty thought for a developing psychology. So I felt I had no choice but to obey the doctrine I implicitly knew was a ridiculous set of rules.

Now here's this guy talking about me being infinite and eternal, and my mind is playing back the hellish, guilt-ridden vision of eternity, and it was making me want to almost gag.

Yet, in the back of my mind, this little voice kept echoing through my consciousness saying, *wait, hold on, really listen to what he's saying, there's something here for you.* So I figured what the hell and I continued to listen, mainly due to the fact that I felt what he was saying in my heart, because otherwise, this shit wasn't making any logical sense.

"Now this circle is ever-present and goes on forever," Filler said as he pointed to each end. "And you, as you may perceive yourself to be in the physical body represents only a portion of this," drawing two vertical lines about five inches apart on top of the circle. "Where you actually are, right now, is in the center," coloring a small dot in the center of the circle.

Pointing to the lines that were five inches apart, "And these two lines represent the birth and death of the physical body. The one on the left, let's say that is when you were born, and the one on the right, let's say that's when you will die. Now the dot in the center, that represents the present moment, right now."

Beginning to see what he was talking about, my mind began to relax its coiled restriction of doubt and defensiveness; opening up to the philosophical foundation of his argument. In that moment my mind relaxed, I realized he wasn't trying to convince me of anything, but rather, simply offering me a perspective I've never seen before.

Continuing on, he began to speak a language that was more familiar to me. "Now in the bible it says we are made in the image," pointing to his chest, "and the likeness of God," as he pointed to his his temple.

"Have any of you ever thought about what the image and likeness of God actually is?" Filler said as a few hands meekly rose. "For most people, these questions are often answered in the early years of childhood and never revisited deeply until and unless a mid-life crisis, a major trauma forces them to, or they take a class such as this. Even then, we as humans often tend to lean towards a comfortable understanding about the most basic questions of life. Or we relegate that responsibility to someone else. We tend to do this because it is more comfortable to the ego.

"It's easiest to assume the most general and superficial understanding as being the absolute of what something actually is. Having absolutes that are dualistic by their very design creates a sense of security. It gives the 'good' guys an 'evil' terrorist to blame. Keeping the question open for reflection and introspection is keeping a desire unquenched. Moreover, if we were to actually realize something that threatened what we thought was right, we take that as a threat to our pride and that would seem to damage the ego."

Filler began to slowly transition from one side of the circle to the other. "It is our natural behavior as humans to devour the unknown; it is the spirit of adventure. It is why we are curious about things. And we like to think we devour the unknown by answering questions. When in actuality, answering questions with dualistic absolutes simply limits our understanding from moving beyond the limits set forth by what we thought was the absolute." Pausing for a moment, professor Filler looked as if he was allowing our minds to absorb the light revealed by sharing his insight.

It was no question that this man was a genius in his own right. Everybody who I had talked to who had taken one of his business classes said "he'll blow your mind." Now sitting there, mind blown, I was beginning to see what they were talking about. And this was only the fourth day of class.

I can't wait to see where this shit goes, this dude's deep... dat's my shit... damn, what the fuck, I'm hangin around Lavont too much, I'm startin to talk like him, I don't say 'dat'.

Turning towards a chair, professor Filler sat down, looked at us with an intense calmness, and said with a tone of curiosity, "What is life?"

Looking around the room, his eyes drifted towards mine, and as our eyes met, a surge of electricity thundered down my spine and I immediately knew he was dead serious about his question. As if how we answered that question had implications there were truly life or death.

Pausing a moment longer, continuing to stare at one another, he began to smile, "Well, what is life?" Breaking the staring contest, he began looking around the room, "Could it be that life is meant to be lived before we could even fathom what it is? What if through actually living life to the fullest we came to see that it is life…the living of it?"

Turning to the right side of the room and staring at the floor, he stood there as if postulating what to say next. "Consider that life is like a tree. A tree, as we know it, springs forth from a seed, and in that seed holds everything that the tree can become," he said, followed by a pause. "Now we can sit here asking 'what is a tree' and as long as we sit there asking, we will never truly come to understand what it is. In order to understand the tree, we must use what it offers. The same can be said about life.

"Imagine you're standing under an apple tree and it's the first time you've seen a tree, let alone an apple tree. Let's say it's your first day on planet earth. Seeing the tree, you ask yourself, 'what is this' and at the same time you ask that question, you begin to notice a sensation of hunger.

"As your attention starts to focus on your experience of hunger, you're no longer concerned about what the tree is. So you start to think of where you can get food to quench the hunger. Now remember, you're standing under an apple tree. Yet, because you're no longer concerned with it, you think it is pointless to stand there any longer, so you begin to search for food, for something familiar, something comfortable. So you turn and walk away from the tree.

"Now not only are you turning away from food to nourish your physical body, the apples, you're turning away from the possibility of quenching the thirst for knowledge. Remember, your original question was asking about what the tree is. And by not eating the fruit of the tree of knowledge, you remain hungry.

"So too in life, when we are confronted with a basic question about life and the answer is staring us in the face, how many times do we turn our back from receiving the fruit of what this grand game has to offer. If we simply ate from the tree of knowledge, instead of complaining about how life sucks and getting caught up in a superficial understanding of egoic compromise, we might gain some clarity. And as you turn your back on the tree, so too do you turn your back on ever coming to an understanding of what it is. Unless you come to again revisit the question.

"If you simply reached up, snatched an apple off the tree, took a bite, and received the blessing; you would realize the truth is there for you to see, you simply have to be Open to receive it," he said with emphasis. After pausing for a moment, he then said, "and be AWAKE to realize it."

Immediately, as he said the word "awake", a few heads snapped up slightly, trying to hide the fact they were dozing. "Simply eating the fruit from the tree, you come to understand that it's a source of nourishment. In the same way that if you receive what life offers you, you'll come to a deeper understanding of life. Through living life and fully exercising the power of our infinite conscious existence, we come to understand our existence more intimately."

Instantly, as the last word left his mouth, it began to echo through my mind, *intimately… intimately… intimacy… intimacy…* My hand shot up as if in an involuntary reaction triggered by that word.

"Yes Michael, you have a question?" Filler responded.

Searching for the words, "Yeah, well, more of an insight slash question really." Unable to form my thoughts into a coherent sentence, I began to speak, consciously moving from one word to the next, "well, its just…its what you said, that last sentence…well actually, the last word, I felt it hit my chest, and it seems so simple, to just live, ya know…to our fullest potential. But how do we know what that is if we don't know who we are or where we came from…I guess what I'm asking is, how do I actually know who I am, beyond all the bullshit my mind tries to make up?"

Professor Filler began to speak slowly, "Well, let's look at it rationally. Based purely on experimentation and observation of what we see in the physical world." As he said that, a sense of trust rang through me as I realized he went to great lengths in contemplating what he was teaching. "Astrophysicists generally agree that our universe was made manifest through what's known as 'The Big Bang.' For reasons still unknown, the Big Bang happened. We don't know why, all we can validly say is that it just did. And when it did, it created the arena that we have come to know as 'space-time' or what is more commonly known as 'the universe.'

"In this universe as we know it, everything is subject to that fundamental framework called space-time, three dimensions of space and one dimension of time, 3 plus 1. All physical laws are subject to the scrutiny of this all-pervasive foundation. The question must be asked," pausing for a moment, "And this is where we get philosophical rather than empirical; the question that must be asked is, what were the conditions that gave rise to the Big Bang, or the physical universe before it existed?"

As if allowing the question to sink in, he cocked his head and raised an eyebrow, gesturing like he wanted us to seriously think about it for moment. "Before the actual Bang occurred, and before the first moment of space-time experience, there had to be a *potential possibility*," he annunciated deliberately, "for it to even arise within the primordial foundation we currently experience as existence. Without a fundamental possibility in the primordial foundation, the Big Bang and this universe would not be possible. In fact, this universe is tuned to such a degree that if it were off by even the slightest, it would not exist. This constancy is called the 'cosmological constant.' If it was not tuned so precisely, the universe as we know it would not exist. Think about that."

Professor Filler, paused, tilted his head to the side as if he was contemplating his next words. "Let me give it to you like this," he said. "The every-thing-ness that is the universe arises from the no-thing-ness that is infinite potential." As soon as he said that, he began to look at me like he was expecting me to say something, "Michael do you have a question?"

Still in my contemplation over what he just said, "Well yeah, wouldn't the infinite potential be that actual everything-ness if it held the potential for everything?"

What was exciting to me was that I was actually following what he was saying. Even more interesting was the fact that I was actually interested in what he was saying. I full-well expected to be asleep during class, it was what I was looking forward to. Yet, here I was in a philosophical conversation about the foundation of the universe. And not only was I interested, I was following his understanding.

And although I was amazed at all that, the most interesting thing was it felt like it was only me and him in the room. Yeah, there were other people in the room, but it felt like they were merely props on a stage so professor Filler and I could act out this scene. It felt like what he was saying was specifically intended for me, like I was the only one in the room that was actually supposed to "get" what he was talking about.

"Nice question," he said, "And ultimately, how you come to answer that question for yourself is a matter of perspective; because at this point in what I'm saying, we are departing from being able to empirically validate that. What I can say is that the field of infinite potential, that substratum of quantum potential where *infinities* tend to linger; that field doesn't necessarily hold any form. It exists as an infinite field where no 'thing' exists, but rather, the simple possibility. In a sense, it is a vast ocean holding only the possibility, not the physical actuality. The actualization of potential into kinetic only arises when the possibility manifests as a reality within your experience.

"You know," he quickly plied on, "A lot of people, and I'm generalizing here when I say people; people tend to think that the Bang of the Big Bang happened all those billions of years ago, and it may very well have. I'm not saying they're wrong. However, a more accurate view might be that it's more like it banged and never stopped banging. It's like a bomb that exploded and never stopped exploding. Just as a bomb needs fuel to sustain its reaction, so too does this universe. That quantum potential, or field of infinite potential, is essentially the fuel that sustains the continued explosion of this universe. Without that fuel, this universe would simply dissipate like the smoke of a bomb.

"I'd even venture to guess there is a central sun of this universe that is that explosion. Just as the sun of this solar system is 'exploding' and providing light to all life in this solar system.

"What's interesting is that the moment to moment experience of life in this physical domain, life as we perceive it, that moment to moment-ness is the explosion and manifestation of infinite possibility into the reality we call 'the physical universe'. And we experience the process of that moment to moment experience as life." Filler paused, "So, to bring it back around in efforts to answer your question Michael, the seed that holds the potential for that tree to become everything that it is, exists just as the infinite field holds the potential for the universe to become everything that it is, and in that is who you are, who I am, who everybody is." He stopped speaking, looked around the room, and then again back at me.

"Let me ask you this," he said, "why is the universe called a uni-verse? Is it because it is unified as one in this particular verse that is in divine source – God? Or is it that its one verse among many in the song that is existence? Or is it both? Or is it neither?

Filler quickly looked at the watch on the wrist, and back up to the all of us sitting, waiting to hear something profound, "And before we end today and do our meditation, let me just say this. Just as the seed of the apple tree sees that it will become an apple tree, and the apple tree sees that it was birthed from that seed of potential; what do you see as your full potential in becoming all that you are when you look into the field of infinite potential that is the future – what is *your* vision you see for life?"

As professor Filler shuffled around, getting the meditation CD ready to play, my mind raced trying to fully comprehend what just happened. Never before had my mind been opened to such a depth in such a short period of time. Sure I was open-minded, but it felt as though the events of the last twelve hours put 50 lbs. of dynamite on the door of my mind and everything that professor Filler said today was like him softly saying "hey Mike, fire in the hole," and now all I saw was a giant gateway between worlds. One full of light and the other full of darkness, all that was left for me to do was to walk through that gateway.

I'd be lying if I said it was an easy decision to take that trip through this seeming stargate between worlds. So I stood there, looking at this gateway in my mind. Awoken from my trance by the sounds of a distant voice giving instructions, readying us to meditate, *How can I meditate, I can't possibly stop thinking about this,* I thought to myself.

Before I knew it, the instructions of his voice and the sounds of the meditation CD had me thoughtless and drifting through an endless sea of clouds until I was standing in front of a giant purple curtain. As I approached the stage that this curtain veiled, I could see the slit where it would open center stage to reveal what was behind it.

I reached with my left hand for the left side that overlapped the right. As my hand touched the curtain I began to hear a low hum of voices on the other side. Now holding the flap, I began to raise it away from the other half, a body-less face floated straight toward mine, reacting, I jumped back.

The face darted behind the right curtain before it reached the opening. Finally noticing I had let go of the flap, I chose not to try and open it again. Instead, I simply stood there and listened. As I stood there, more faces began to protrude, first one, then two, then five, as if trying to come through the curtain only showing an impression of the face, creating a vacuum sealed impression with the curtain.

By this time, I began to hear the verbal cues to begin associating my awareness with the sensation of the physical body. I wiggled my toes and fingers, slowly moving my appendages until fully back in the awareness of my body. Sitting there, dumbfounded, I realized there was no way I could comprehend what just happened to me, *I need to talk to professor Filler, this shit's too crazy for me to figure out on my own.*

Chapter 3 – After Class

Waiting, watching and half listening to the few people still lingering after class, my mind rolled through thought after thought. And yet, I sat there with an excitement emerging from my bones and coursing throughout my body. It was a new experience for me, feeling excitement course through my body like it was. Yet it was a natural peace, like this peaceful excitement was embedded deep within me as an authentic and basic feeling to my being human.

The feeling was something I had long since forgotten about, and now, clearing away the mists of my mind. I was starting to remember. And it felt more real than anything I've known since I was a young child, of no more than four years old, playing without a care in the world.

Watching the last person say good-bye to professor Filler, she turned to walk away. As she did, Filler glancing at me, smirked, turned and walked towards his desk. As he walked, he spoke, "So Michael, how was class today, d'ya learn anything?"

Did I learn anything, is this guy serious, I thought. "Yeah, it was good. Interesting, definitely something to consider." I wasn't going to let on too much, I had to keep my wits, keep my cards hidden until I felt I could reveal my hand. "Hey, you mind if I ask you a question. I've kinda had a strange day, and I remember you talkin about somethin called synchronicity, and I guess I just feel I need to talk to someone, and you're about the only person that comes to mind."

"Well," he said, looking like he was thinking about it. "I have some time right now, or later today, which do you prefer?"

"Right now's good for me."

Sitting down in his chair and closing his leather organizer. "Alright then, whatcha got?"

Where do I start, I thought as I grabbed a chair from a nearby table, put it in front of me and sat down. "Uh, well, it all really started this morning with a dream I had. Then during class today things were just different, and I'm ... I'm not really sure how to start."

"How about the beginning?" he said.

"Yah, that's an obvious place. So, I guess, the dream." Taking a deep breath to begin what I knew was going to be a long conversation, "Well," I released the breath. "It was crazy, it was unlike any dream I've ever had ... kinda like it was real life, it just hasn't happened yet ... like I was seein the future or something ... in the dream, I was talkin to my dead cat who isn't actually dead yet, but in the dream, he said he was dead and giving the people reading the book I haven't written yet the back story of my life," I said forcing out the final words as the air in my lungs quickly emptied.

"Anyway, I was readin this book, and this whole first chapter was talkin about my past, and my future, but I was looking back on it, on the future that I haven't actually experienced yet. So it was like I was in the future looking back on my past, but it's a past that is my future.

"And it was my cat Charlie doing the talkin, and he took me back to some, well, interesting times of my past."

Filler smiled, and said, "Is there more."

"Yeah ... so that was the dream ... what's weird is, I know I don't know shit about what that book was talkin about, at least not yet. But the thing about it was, that the dream was more like a memory of a future thing that's gonna occur ... like I was actually readin the book, and it felt nothing like a dream, but like, reality, like me and you sittin here talkin. It felt like this," I said as I pointed to him, and then back to myself. As I said that, professor Filler leaned back in his chair, a small smile cracked across his face. Continuing to look at my eyes, I could sense he knew where this was going.

I continued on, "Then, as I come in here today, I figured it was gonna be a regular class. But, no, I sit down and things get crazy all over again. Long story short, everything that you were sayin today, felt like it was downloading into my mind, into my consciousness. Like I could feel all the data come in through my forehead and become a part of me, it was ... it was really weird.

"Then, during meditation, I went to a place with a purple curtain, like the ones that are on theatre stages, ya know? I tried to open the curtain, I cracked it and a ghost-like face came out at me, then I saw other faces, tryin to like, come through the curtain or somethin... like I said, it was weird, just plain weird. And I have no idea what to make of all of this other than it was important that it happened."

Sitting there, still perplexed, I watched and waited for him to respond. But he just sat there, looking at his leather organizer, then another smile came across his face as he looked up at me, "I wonder who those people were behind the curtain. Think you'll ever get to meet 'em?"

My mind jumped back in reaction, *What, what the fuck, what is this guy asking me ... what kind of question is that?*

He began to speak again, "Dreams are highly symbolic, and really, there is no definitive interpretation, except, within your own consciousness. I could sit here and tell you anything you wanted to know about the symbolism of your dreams, but it's pointless, because all the symbols used in your dreams pertain specifically to your life. Yeah, there are universal symbols, but for the most part, you have to listen to that voice in you when it comes to dreams. Did you write it down?"

"Nah. But what about it feelin like it was real?" I asked.

"What does that mean to you?" he asked back.

"I don't know, maybe it's real or it will be real, or some shit like that?" I said, unsure of anything at this point.

"That's an interpretation," Filler said. "The thing you have to consider is that nobody really knows what dreams fully do; they do a lot of different things. For the most part, though, they're messages. Messages for you and your life, to help You guide You," he said with emphasis. "Ultimately, it's really not all that important that you understand the symbols, your consciousness already does. The best thing you could do is just write the dreams down in a journal, then come back to it and read it one day when your mind has had time to absorb it and move on.

"When you do come back to it, just listen to that voice in the back of your head, or pay attention to any visions and feelings that you get when you're reading it that have importance to you. There will be something there when you read back through it. It's not necessary to force yourself to understand your dreams, just allow your intuition to be the guide. That's mostly what dreams are, an extension of your intuition," he said as he uncrossed his legs and then re-crossed with his legs in the opposite position as before.

I paused for a moment to think about what he said before responding, "Yeah, I can understand that … but, what about rationality, and deducing things into easily understandable bits of knowledge? Couldn't I deduce what all the symbols mean to me, and then juxtapose that with my dream?"

"You could, and if you want to do that, by all means, go ahead. But it's really not necessary. Do you know the main distinction between logic and intuition as sources for guidance in making decisions for our lives?" He asked as he picked up his pen.

"Not really, no," I said as looked at the pen in his hands.

"Take this pen, for example, let's say this is you." Holding the pen by the cap, it dangled vertically out the tips of his thumb and index finger. "This pen can see only so far to the left and to the right, and only so far up and so far down before the distance of the direction it's looking becomes too great to fully understand anything it's looking at. Outside of this sphere of *close proximity* of which the pen can see, the logical or rational mind cannot truly understand anything. Because it has to deal with the many variables in its face, and cannot make sound judgment about something far off in the distance, like, the future, even tomorrow's future is too far off for the rational mind to be absolutely sure of what *is*. There are generalities it can assume as constant, but certainty can only be derived from this present moment.

"Now, it's important to say that rationality has its place, but it's more for understanding things from what is known. And it cannot be the overall guidance to ones happiness because there are too many variables it has to contend with to see where true happiness lies.

"Intuition on the other hand, can see it all. Using intuition to guide your life is like someone reading you the directions to your life, and logic is like trying to reverse engineer your life without ever having taken it apart to begin with. Your logical human mind cannot grasp anything outside that frame of reference, or context it has built throughout your life. Your intuition exists beyond the horizon of that context, and can see everything within it. But, don't get me wrong, you must know how to listen to your intuition before it can be of use to you. Do you see what I'm sayin?"

Sitting there as he continued talking, my mind drifted off from his words, I was unsure of what he was getting at, I had never really thought of intuition as a guiding voice in my actions. I just always did what I thought I should be doing. For the past year or so, rational thought had become a large part of the way I guided my actions.

At least that's what you tell yourself, you know damn well you don't base anywhere near the large part of your actions on rational thought … what about smokin weed when you're in the military, is that a rational fucking choice? a voice in my mind said, interrupting my thoughts.

Immediately, I was again focused on what professor Filler was saying.

"Understand that everything we witness and observe *in* the physical world, is a series of effects, none the true cause, none. The observable evidence of the world, or how something appears to be, is the last stage of the existence of the actual thing we are observing. It's like watching an old man before his death. All physical world observations are like watching that old man take his last breath. The true cause exists as choice that emerges from infinite potential. Your choice is the gateway for the true cause to exert its power in your life. The series of events are effects of that cause. On top of that, everything you see out there," Filler pointing out the window, "It's already a past circumstance.

"There is a time delay on the perceived observable world, just like when you're watching a football game on Sunday, there's about a twenty-five second time delay between when it actually happens, and when you see it on your TV screen. The same thing happens in the perceived world, except, the time delay is significantly reduced. It takes time for light to enter your eye and time for that signal and information your eye picks up to send it to your brain to be processed, and it takes time for your brain to process it. Then, after all that has already happened, your mind must understand it according to the context you have built in your mind that is what you think you know; and in that, there's a huge lag time in using logical thinking for in the moment decisions."

"Wait a second," I interrupted. "You're sayin that everything I perceive in the physical world is already in the past?"

"Yes, that's exactly what I'm saying," he said matter-of-fact like. "It must be understood that using logic as the trump card in guiding your decision is basing the decision entirely upon that split second moment of observable evidence that is already in the past, as you observe it. Anybody that has played sports and has been any good at all, knows that if you have to logically think about your next move, while you're in the heat of action actually making the moves, you're done before you've even started. You ever heard of being in the zone?"

"Yeah," I answered.

"Ask a teammate about what they were thinking at a time when they were in the zone, I guarantee they'll say something to the effect, 'I don't know, I just … did it.' Being in the zone is similar to the ancient eastern philosophy and paradox called wei-wu-wei, or 'effortless doing.' If you're always trying to rationalize your actions, you will always be rationalizing, and never be experiencing the current moment for what it is."

"I think I see what you're talking about," I said. "Intuition guides, and rational thought clarifies. Is that pretty much what you're saying?" I asked as I sat forward in my chair while shifting over to the right side.

"More or less, yeah," Filler said while starring at his leather organizer. "Michael, can I just speak for a moment, I feel like I need to say something to you and I'm not quite sure what it is, so I, I just want to … just want to channel something, for lack of a better term."

Dumbstruck by his request, "Yeah … I guess so. I'll just listen."

"Remember the old man analogy I was just talking about?"

"Yeah," I acknowledged while slightly shaking my head yes.

"To understand that old man, and let's say that the old man represents your reality," he paused, "To come to a full understanding of the old man, or your reality, you must take that wholly subjective perspective, and objectify it by breaking it all down to the essence of what is, in this case, the entire life of the old man AND that which gives rise to the old man even existing in the first place.

"Then you must embrace the total state of that man, mentally, physically, emotionally and spiritually in order to arrive at the true cause, which is, in every case, the potentiality of the life of the old man in that which exists as infinite possibility. Infinite possibility being that which gives rise to the very existence of what you are observing, that is, the old man, or in your case, the reality you perceive all around you.

"The interesting thing to note is that the process of unifying the subjective and objective is what is called forgiveness. And through the process of forgiveness, your reality, mental, emotional, physical, and spiritual state of existence dramatically shifts to a clearer dimensional viewpoint of reality.

"How reality appears to exist in your mind must be observed from both a subjective and an objective standpoint in the same moment if you are to truly understand the dynamics at work in your life. You didn't just show up in this *moment* out of nowhere, and you didn't just show up in this *reality* out of nowhere. So what is the seed of potential that gives rise to the spirit that exists within you?" He said, pausing a moment, still starring at the leather organizer.

He then continued, "Here's a key, once you have objectified your subjectively logical analysis of the situation, you have to unify that seeming dichotomy and duality into oneness.

"There is no real objectivity or subjectivity; they are only aspects of how your consciousness operates within your perceived reality. Forgiveness is that process of unification. To take each aspect and turn it into the other, you will see that there is no clear distinction between the two. They are merely a way, or mode of perceiving things. They are not fundamental existence. Both objectivity and subjectivity are processes your mind uses to come to know itself. I'm sure you've heard of the observer becoming the observed and the observed being the observer. Same thing," he said, pausing for a moment, then continuing, "You with me so far?" He said now looking at me.

"For the most part," *this is fuckin crazy shit*, I thought. "Just keep goin," I said as he looked back to the leather organizer and then back at me.

"Alright," he said with a smile, "When you observe something, say you witness an accident, when you observe that accident, your understanding of that situation is entirely wrapped up in how you perceive the circumstances of the situation. How you perceive it is what's known as your perspective.

"Your perspective is entirely built up by your beliefs. Your beliefs are an entirely subjective agreement that filters this thing called reality. This is known as your contextual frame of reference. Even if your beliefs are founded in scientific fact, they are still an agreement by the *subject* who agrees to them. Your beliefs are an agreement by the subject, you, thus begetting a subjective agreement. A choice, based from the position YOU observe YOUR contextual frame of reference.

"Have you ever seen two people witness the same exact thing," he said. "I'm talking, the exact same series of events. Then they walk away with two totally different descriptions and understandings of what happened? It happens every day, everywhere you go, and it's not that it's necessarily wrong or bad. It's simply people choosing to be who they think they are. And who they think they are is generated by the matrix, or system of beliefs they have agreed to over the course of their lives.

"Who you are, Michael, the one before me right now, is the One behind all action, and as you have arrived here today, you walked through the culmination of every choice you have made in life. The question you have to ask yourself is, what is 'it' that provides the possibility for you to even exist as you exist right here and now? What are the prime conditions that gives rise to the being you know as *me*, in this moment, right now? Think about it for a second."

Filler paused, watching me with intent. A minute or so later, he said, "For lack of a better term, that primal source that gives rise to you is your soul. And that soul arises from the very Spirit that Michael truly is. The center and source beyond who you know yourself to be. And that, that is who you truly are. The key is to move beyond the horizon of circumstantial evidence of who you 'think' you are, if you truly want to realize the fundamental essence beyond who you think you are," he said. Pausing for a moment before glancing up and into my eyes, he smiled and looked back to the leather organizer.

A peaceful silence filled the air for several moments. He continued on, "Listen, beliefs are beliefs; nobody is right or wrong in coming to choose, or agree to what they believe. Beliefs are simply attractor patterns that harmonize into your reality whatever it is you want to experience for as long as you hold that belief. They are like a software program that operates your hardware that is composed of an infinite conscious existence, or freedom. Your awareness is the one that shines light and creates a conscious existence that radiates onward into infinity. All your cognitive abilities and behaviors are subject to the scrutiny of the filter that is your beliefs."

"Yeah!" I said as I lurched forward in my chair with the realization that my dream was saying the same thing. "That's what my cat was saying in my dream, self- reflection, or knowing thyself, as they say. Though he was a helluva lot more cryptic about it."

Filler paused again, then looking up from the organizer and into my eyes, he said, "If you truly want to make a difference in the reality of your life, pop the cork of your beliefs that's constraining the flow of your very source, your primal awareness. When you do that, you'll see the reality of the condition-less essence that gives rise to your existence, and it floods in as the ever-present realization of your fundamental essence." As he paused, an awkward silence filled the air as he continued to look at me.

Unable to bear the silence, I spoke, "That all sounds good and everything, but how do you do that? How do you 'pop the cork?'"

Taking a moment, he then said, "Well, you first must accept that the circumstances of the world are not the foundation of who you are, your One true identity. How the world appears to be, all of it, those circumstances are impermanent and merely effects. They come and go and are as transient as the wind. When speaking in terms of eternal ever-lasting truth, anything that changes is not fundamentally real, it is merely an illusion, a mist, clouding the clarity of the sun of your ever-living soul.

"With that being said, if you base the reality of who you are on anything that is not eternal, you are clouded in the illusion of appearances.

"However, when you come to open towards the light of your eternal self, you are then founded in the true reality of ever-lasting significance. Nothing will ever truly change in your experience until you accept at least that much, otherwise you are simply changing one transient and subjective motivation for another, on and on, lifetime after lifetime, until you're eventually no longer limited by vanity and egoic pride," he said as he shifted in the chair, uncrossing and re-crossing his legs.

"Let me give you an example Michael. There is a woman I know, who once commented that everything I just told you 'sounded nice,' just as you did, then she said to me, 'but I just don't think you are in reality.'

"She went on to describe her reality. Single mother, no man to help her, bills piling up, no money, and it was Christmas time too, and she didn't have money for presents either. She also commented that she likes to fix herself up and look good because it makes her feel better, she also said she's always having to deal with guys calling late at night for a rendezvous of sorts, and that it was kind of annoying.

"So this is what she explained to me as her reality, then she took it one step further and said, 'imagine what it's like for me, put yourself in my shoes.' Now, bear with me here. Her situation, 'my reality' as she says, it is what it is – the bills, the kids, all that.

"All of those things are circumstances of life brought about through a very long chain of choices that string back throughout the entirety of time, and they flow through her system of interpreting reality, or her beliefs. If her parents wouldn't have met, her body wouldn't exist in those specific circumstances. So yes, even the very fact that she, you, and I are even alive in this reality is all circumstantial, and if you go to any court of law, circumstantial evidence doesn't prove anything. It can be overwhelming evidence, but it's all still circumstantial, it is all indirect evidence.

"The circumstances – the bills, the kids – all that, it doesn't prove anything, it doesn't prove that it's reality, it may be an aspect or characteristic of how she's perceiving reality, but it's miniscule in the grand scheme of things. And it's still only a perception. Now that may sound offensive and down right uncompassionate to some, but consider the grand scheme.

"Eventually, your life, my life, and her life, at least the circumstances, will eventually become a faded memory. The thing you have to understand is that the circumstances come and go; they are as a snowflake in a lifetime of blizzards.

"The only way circumstances become what seems to be your reality, is when you stake your identity upon them, when you claim personal investment in those circumstances. When that happens, when you stake your identity on a circumstance, effect, or result, you are staking who you know yourself to be on that snowflake that in time becomes water, then vapor, then maybe, back to a snowflake.

"Where do think the term 'identity crisis' comes from? The only way you can have a crisis with your identity is if you have identified the reality of who you are on an impermanent foundation. That is why egoic pride is a limitation. It is the adhesive that keeps you stuck identifying yourself in a relative reality of impermanence and illusion, where you must continually fight off threats to your identity and pride. And fear becomes the controller of your life, and you are forever stuck in fight or flight, and you will never know peace, true peace, lasting peace.

"The type of peace that is founded in an existence not of this world of impermanence; and you will NEVER know it until you relax your vanity to move beyond your own self-imposed context that comes from you thinking your right about anything, or wrong, for that matter."

Leaning forward, professor Filler ignited a laser-like stare into my eyes and began speaking with a commanding voice, "Look to the light of your inner awareness to realize your freedom. Everything you see in the world, everything, it is all sourced to exist from a dimension beyond the constraints of time and impermanence, and most importantly, it exists as a place your limited mind cannot conceive.

Leaning back in his chair, he said, "To realize your true peace and freedom, you must follow the cord of your inner light back to its source, and you do that by becoming aware of everything you can possibly become aware of, and you will see it as a manifestation of your inner world. Everything you perceive 'out there' must first flow through your consciousness from the source that gives you the ability to perceive, that ability to sense. The perception of everything you see 'out there' emanates from an awareness *in here*.

"That awareness, that light, that is who you truly are, and *that*, that is what exists beyond time, and does not change. You will forever be light. Even on a physical level, at the most basic and fundamental level we can conceive, we are composed entirely of light."

Sitting back into his chair, pausing, looking again at the organizer, then up at me, he began to speak with a softness, "Let me give it to you like this, every moment of your existing experience on this earth compiles and forms to create the context and belief program you filter and interpret this reality through. You must realize that the program of your mind is not truth, it simply filters truth. Truth is the fundamental stream from which all existence arises, this fundamental stream could be called God, but in the end, God as you conceive it in the mind is just a concept identified by a label. Neither the label nor the concept can even come close to what they are attempting to explain.

"And, if this is the case, arise from the depths of the dream and pierce the veil of illusion you have for so long conceived of as your reality." Pausing for a moment, professor Filler's eyes locked on mine, and with a slight twitch he straightened his head, "Alright Michael, I think I'm done talking for a moment."

I couldn't move. I felt like I needed to acknowledge him in some way, or at least what he had just said. "Uhm," I said speechless, "I," still speechless, "okay, I'm not sure how to respond to that."

I just sat there starring at this man who was obviously not of this world, like he had beamed down from outer space somewhere. *This guy is fucking ridiculous, like, in the greatest way possible. Who the fuck is this guy,* I thought to myself as I continued to stare at him. "Hey, uh …" unable to say anything else, I just sat there, still speechless. My mind felt numb, like it had just been massaged with a soothing caress until all the knots had melted, and now I just sat there, starring at him, watching him expand his stomach and chest in a slow, long, deep breaths.

Continuing to stare at his leather organizer, "You know Michael, you may not believe this, but I feel there is more I need to say to you. I don't know why it feels so important for me to say all this, but, I just have to." As he finished speaking, he looked up, straight into my eyes, and as he did it felt like his stare came straight in my eyes and down my body, hitting my heart like a blast furnace igniting it with an intense fire.

Still unsure how to respond, "I don't know what you're about to say, but, uh, just say it." The more I tried to wrap my mind around the entire day, the more my mind rejected it, *I have got to be in the fucking twilight zone, there is no way any of this shit is actually my life. What the fuck is happening to me... I'm losin my God Damn mind is what it is.* I began laughing to myself, thinking of the ridiculousness of my current situation. *I fell asleep in a sane fucking reality, and dreamed my ass into the twilight zone, now I don't know where the fuck I am.*

Sliding the leather organizer to the side of the table with a swipe, he began to speak, "Okay, let me give to you like this. Everything is energy; everything you see is literally energy. The table, the chair, the door; everything, it's all energy vibrating. At the most basic levels of reality we know we have atoms. Atoms are essentially balls of energy. For the most part, they have a positive charge, a negative charge and a neutral charge. Now, this energy has certain qualities. An electric aspect, and a magnetic aspect. Electricity creates light, that's how we see it, it lights up."

Filler, making a fist with one hand and taking the index finger of his other, he stuck his finger through the hole made by the thumb and index finger of his fisted hand. "That atom is composed of energy. That energy is sourced from somewhere though, so you have to ask the question, where?

"Well, here's the thing. In order to know where it comes from, you have to look at all the aspects of the energy. And in order to do that, you have to look at both the positive and negative from a neutral position. From within the center of that sphere of energy originates its existence. Just like the sun providing all life in our solar system, without the sun you would have no *solar* system. The sun is what makes it solar. And just like in an atom, without the nucleus, there would be no atom. You also have to know, that what I'm saying is just an analogy, so don't get all caught up in its ineffectiveness to accurately explain everything, no analogy can for they are merely symbols or signposts that lead to the truth.

"Anyway, let's make it personal now. The body you are experiencing is composed of a great deal of atoms, and those atoms are composed of energy. So on a physical level, the body is pure energy. And again, the question is where does that energy come from? Well, to know that, you have to look at where you originate from, and to do that you have to look at your center, your core, and to do that you have to look within.

"Let's say you're a fiber in a bundle of fiber optics. Looking outside of yourself would be, as if you were trying to figure out where *your* light was coming from by looking at another fiber in your bundle. It'd be like you asking another fiber, 'hey, where does your light come from?' And the other fiber, let's call him George, he would say, 'I don't know, never really thought about it, I think my light might come from that fiber over there, he seems to know what's goin on, he must be our salvation.' So you and George go and listen to what the other fiber in your bundle has to say, he says, 'the kingdom of God is within you.' And you and George look at this fiber like he's the greatest thing in the world, and don't really listen to what he's sayin. All the while, he's sayin, 'I AM the light of the world, the kingdom of God is *within* you, it does not come with careful observation, it is within you, and when you *seek ye first the kingdom*, all things will be added unto you, *you* are the light of the world, let *your* light shine before men, ask and it will be given to you, seek and you will find it, knock and the door will be opened to you.' You see what I'm saying?" Filler asked.

Taking a quick deep breath, he continued, "Now you and George sit there like he's the Son of God and you're not, even after he says 'the kingdom of God is within you'. When in all actuality your light is sourced from a central processor that is all sourced from the same place. Not only is your light sourced from within, but your fiber is composed of atoms that are composed of light. Do you see what I'm getting at here?" he asked

I could see where he was going, but I had to question his argument. "Uh, yeah, but what difference does it make, if I'm light, I'm light. Ashes to ashes, dust to dust, isn't that what they say? If I'm light, I'll realize it someday, no matter how many cycles of ashes and dust it takes to do so, isn't that what reincarnation talks about?"

"Well yeah, basically. But remember Michael, why are you here listening to these words? Why are you having this strange day with that crazy dream you had? You asked me about synchronicity when you first sat down, so what is the relevance of everything I'm saying combined with everything you're experiencing? Why are you still sitting here, talking to me about all this, listening to these words, what is the relevance of all of that? Is it merely a coincidence? Why do I feel like it's important for you to be hearing these words? If you've noticed, I haven't been acting exactly normal. Is it that all this is just a 'glitch in the matrix?'?"

As he finished speaking, my body seized up, I couldn't move. The enormity of what he had just said hit my mind like a bolt of lightning snapping its power right outside the window. Something was definitely happening to me, I just didn't know what. And as I sat there motionless, the entire day flashed in my mind causing me to turn from its brightness.

"Professor, I don't know what the hell is happening, all I know is that it is, where its leading is still yet to be revealed. Like I've been on the same path for so long and now I've gotten lost in the woods and I can't find my way out. And then today happened, and it's like the trees that were rooted in my mind for so long are uprooting and clearing a path for me. It's a path I haven't taken before, that much is so obvious it's ridiculous. But the journey, I know is leading to a place of something profound. I don't know what that is, I don't know where it is, I don't know how it is, I just know it is… I just know."

Breaking off my stare-down with Filler, I looked out the window at the snow falling softly, one flake after another, and it reminded me of peace. Each flake not caring about where it was headed, just falling with beauty and grace until it came to a rest, sitting one atop another, blanketing the once green lushness that was sprinkled with flowers and birds singing melodic tunes.

But now the snow, so peaceful and quiet took me to my childhood, spending hours digging out tunnels in the snowdrifts on the farm. There was no big concern back then, just joy. Not worried about my career or what's right and what's wrong, just the enjoyment of being alive and living in the moment.

All that fun, that joy seemed so distant for so long, like I was supposed to be somehow different in some way than I was when I was a child, and it didn't make sense anymore.

"Michael," professor Filler said, breaking my daydream. "Michael, you're obviously in a transformational process right now, and you will experience things that your mind cannot understand, for you have never experienced them before, possibly not even in your past lives. The key is to unite all things. Whatever seems to be a duality in your mind; unite it. Break it down to its most fundamental essence through forgiveness, and move forward on that deep understanding. Forget what things may look like, appearances are appearances, the reality is never what it seems to be," he said.

"But it's so hard," I said "not to get wrapped up in all that shit, it's everywhere. It's what drives society, tryin to make shit appear to be something that it's not. How can I exist in that type of world and be the me that doesn't give a shit about all that?" I said, almost in tears.

"Look, I can't tell you what to do anymore than I know where your path leads, I don't. All I can do is offer you what I can, and you will have to make the decision for your own life, it is what life's all about, making the choice. Realize that you have a great opportunity right now. You see all this, and you can make a choice that has the potential to make your life and the lives of many others everything you dreamed it could be, and so much more. I have more that I want to tell you, but if you feel that you need to take some time, we can always talk later."

Nah, I'm here, if I leave now ... no, fuck that, I thought to myself. "No, I'm here now, I can sort through it later," I said while starring at his leather organizer.

"Well then, if we can go back to what we were talking about earlier, I'd want to clarify it for ya," he said.

"Yeah, that's cool, it's whatever."

"So," he said, pausing for a moment, "let's join the metaphor together. Say your physical body is a fiber of fiber optics and you have this light running through you. And the very reason you know that is because you're aware; you are aware that you are aware. You see what I'm sayin?

"Now let's say you're somebody that's only concerned about the appearances and how the results look, or what you look like, and how much money you have, and having a bigger house than your neighbor, or bigger rims on your car, or the newest phone on the market, or whatever it is.

"That would be like a fiber optic being more concerned about the gossip that's takin place on a phone conversation than actually doin its job. Its Job is to be a conduit of light. Now you may be wondering what the ego is. Well, it's the fiber thinking it's something other than the light that it really is, and if you don't realize that not only is your light sourced from a central unified light, but that you are the light, it's unfortunate to say, but you will know suffering to be your reality. And again, it's all a choice to perceive the reality that you're thinking as real to be as such. In other words, the thoughts you think that have you think you know what reality is and who you are, are the thoughts that you're thinking you think you know.

"You see, if you didn't have the light running through you, you wouldn't be aware of the fact that you have the awareness of light running through you. Just like a fiber would not be aware of its light if it didn't have light running through it, the light is the source of life. Without it, there is no life.

"The very fact that you're aware of your awareness is enough to say that you have light running through you. Just like on a cold dark night you need a flashlight to see around. The light from the bulb gives you the ability to see where you are going, and without that light, you struggle to find your way around. Until eventually, you stub your toe on something, and now you're suffering.

"Looking within gives you the ability to not only see, and know, that you and everything else is light, but it also gives you the ability to express how much light you want to shine. Have you ever heard, 'we are made in the image and likeness of God?' Considering that our light is sourced from somewhere, what else is the 'source' other than God? And how much 'likeness' do we hold?

"If God is the source of existence, do *we* then source the perception of everything that occurs within our personal awareness? If God is the source of light, and we are made in the image and likeness, of that source of light, and we can see that we are aware of our light, and we know that everything is composed of light... is it possible that we have the power to create the image of everything we think we see in our awareness?

"The image of anything; the table, the door, the chair, it's all light and we have these things that filter light called eyeballs.

We also have this thing that filters the information called a brain, and we have this thing that controls the amount of energy we give to the light called a heart. And here's the thing, we have our experiences that gives us our perspective which tends to dominate our beliefs, which then controls our thoughts, which then controls our words and actions, which then controls our habits, which then controls our character, which then controls our destiny. And all the while, we're worried about our image, and how things appear.

"Well, I hate to break it to ya, the image of what you think you are is controlled by your ego, because it is your ego, and you're just scratching the surface of who you actually are when you question that identity. And who you truly are, well, you're an infinite source of all light in the universe. And you're worried what color of shirt to wear and what rims accessorize your car the best, or what suit to wear to the party. Which is fine and all, I'm just sayin, you can choose your destiny, the fate of your life and everything in the world, and you're concerned about rims on a car.

"All you have to do is look within and you will see your light, not only that, you will see that you are that light, and as such you will see that you have the power of that light. Why? Because you are that power, and you shine your light and use your power however you allow yourself to. How? Well that is something you will discover when you embrace the willingness to open to honest and transparent expression.

"Here's the importance of everything I'm telling you Michael. You have the power to choose anything you want to experience. How? Because *it* is *your* experience, and you control how you experience things by the conscious use of your existence. And when you look within and realize you are light, that looking within gives energy to everything you see because you see everything as that light. And you'll also realize that the vision you choose to see determines what you see as the context of your life. In that, you will understand that you create your experience by how you see your experience and how open your magnetic nature is to giving. This giving energy is felt in emotions, and emotions are in certain ways, a volitional input into what you see. And this dynamic creates the reality of the experience that you are experiencing.

"You see what I'm getting at here? Your mind controls the image of what you see, and your heart controls the power behind what you see, which then creates the reality of your experience. The experience is what you know to be life in this physical domain. And when you *know* life to be light, you will know that you already walk in heaven because heaven is all around you, and as you see it, you see it everywhere. You will also understand that the hell in which you used to live, with all the suffering, you will know it to be an illusion. That darkness is only a veil, a mirage that keeps you in fear, afraid to pierce through the void between the surface of your world and the center that is your source.

"You see, fear is only the illusion that says you can be threatened, and it plays out as the darkness and evil you see, and terror you feel. The illusion isn't real, it's all an idea you have built up in your mind about why you shouldn't pierce the void and look within. You'll think you'll be wrong about everything and you won't dare hurt your own pride.

"Who cares if your wrong, big deal, it was all an illusion anyway, and when you see the light, it won't be any concern to you regardless of what you think is right or wrong.

"Love is all there is. Light is all there is. Light is your mind and Love is your heart. You have the power to shine your light and feel love everywhere. How? By giving your love and light unconditionally and unceasingly to everything.

"No limitations, no restrictions, no constraints. Why do you think it's called Unconditional Love? Because you must give it, before you even think about putting conditions on it. Giving it before you do that is the process called Forgiveness, you might try it sometime. It's how you become a conduit of pure light and love.

"I know you may doubt everything that I'm saying, and it's okay, it's really nothing to be concerned about. In deed, it is better to not believe and find out for yourself.

"Life is both a blessing and a lesson. A blessing because it's a lesson, and a lesson because it's a blessing. It's your duty in being human, to realize your potential. You know what that last statement means right, 'to realize your potential?'"

"Nah," I said. "Well, maybe to see the truth of who I am?"

"In a sense, yeah... and with that, before you leave, let me give you two quotes to think about."

"Alright."

"The first comes from the Gospel of Thomas," Filler paused for a moment, "Jesus said, 'If those who lead you say,

'See, the Kingdom is in the sky,' then the birds of the sky will precede you. If they say to you, 'It is in the sea,' then the fish will precede you. Rather, the Kingdom is inside of you, and it is outside of you. When you come to know yourselves, then you will become known, and you will realize that it is you who are the sons of the living Father. But if you will not know yourselves, you dwell in poverty and it is you who are that poverty."

"What does it mean Michael, to come to know your self? Just contemplate upon it, there's no need to answer."

"What's the second quote," I asked.

"It's comes from Osho," Filler said, "an Indian philosopher, who once said, 'Drop the idea of becoming someone, because you are already a masterpiece. You cannot be improved. You have only to come to it, to know it, to realize it. God himself has created you, you cannot be improved.'"

Chapter 4 - Reflection

Quietly sitting in the computer lab, staring at the words on the monitor, the flood of insight continued to drown everything I thought I knew, replacing it with an intense light my rational mind could not understand.

After just having sat through the most intense class I've ever had, that was preceded by the most visceral dream I've ever had, my mind was still not ready to grasp the imperative nature of everything that was flooding my mind. *I have got to be goin fuckin insane … I'm crazy, I've literally gone fuckin insane, there is no way that this is reality … no fuckin way.*

It has always been my default way of being, that if I didn't understand something, I would research it. And although I somehow understood what professor Filler was saying, I could not allow myself to believe it. Yet, there was something in me that knew there was a mountain of truth to what he was saying. I simply was not allowing myself to accept it.

And now, as I read the bible quote, I felt the words hit my heart like a hammer. Cracking the shell it had been encased in, as a warmth began to permeate my body. And the words I just read seeped into every cell, *you are the light of the world, let your light shine … YOU are the light of the world, let YOUR light shine … let your light shine … you are the light … shine, let your light shine.*

These words continued echoing through my mind and body as a shower of chills ran down my spine. An intense light began filling every crevice and crack of my brain. Immediately, my entire life made sense. Yet, I sat there, believing I was the most insane person on planet earth.

I am Christ, my mind quietly whispered. *WHAT THE FUCK? This doesn't make sense … what, the fuck, is happening to me. NO … no way I'm the reincarnation of Jesus fucking Christ,* I blasted back to the whispering voice in my mind telling me I was the Christ. *That's just not fucking possible.*

Again, my spine began sparkling with chills, this time more intense than the last, *I have to be though, life doesn't make any sense otherwise.* I couldn't accept the conclusion my mind was offering me, *NO FUCKING WAY … no fuckin … no, no, NO FUCKIN WAY. That's … NO … but … but yes, it has to be.*

I gotta do something to take my mind off this shit. I couldn't take the torment of my own insanity anymore. And whenever I needed to focus on something other than my life, basketball was the answer. The form, the technique, the fundamentals of the game are so precise, yet so fluid, that whenever I practice my shot, all my attention and awareness is on expressing perfection-in-motion through my shot. Nothing else can creep in to disturb that peace. Basketball is the one thing that has been my savior through life's ups and downs.

By this time in my life, I had developed my skills enough to play on pretty much any court. Being that I'm 6'7 tends to help, but I know my talent has more to do with all the countless hours I've spent with a basketball in my hands specifically working on mastering my strengths, and strengthening my weaknesses.

Making my way from the computer lab to the gym, I stood there at the free throw line, everything my mind had previously been on faded as if it didn't matter anymore. My mind was again still. *Perfect … perfect … perfect,* I repeated as I took my routine three dribbles. *Perfect … perfect … perfect,* eyeing the little piece of metal at the front of the rim that held the net. *Perfect … perfect … perfect,* positioning my hands. *Elbow in … loose wrist … finish high … feel it … feel it … feel it.*

As if by command, my legs began flexing as I rose through the motion of the shot to the tips of my toes, releasing the ball, watching everything slow down, as time, creeping from moment to moment, became irrelevant. Seeing out of the top of my peripheral vision, the horizontal lines on the ball slowly spun down from top to bottom, one over the other as I continued eyeing the rim.

Slowly the ball approached the rim. Closer and closer, until my perception of time snapped back to normal as the ball sailed untouched through the rim, popping the net as it exited through the bottom.

A deep breath spontaneously arose in my lungs as a soft soothing calmness flowed down my chest, stomach, and then legs. *Peace*, I said to myself, standing at the line, watching the ball hit the floor and bounce back my way from the rotation of the release. Still standing there, not moving, the ball bounced into my cupped hands, and nothing else mattered. It was me, the gym, the ball and my shot. I was finally in the serenity of my world. All silent, save the soothing sounds of the ball caressing the floor on every bounce. Kissing the sweet lips of the bottom of the net. Gliding its every molecule along the sinews of the net's opening – "sploot" – the net would say as it rose in orgasmic excitation from the ball entering and exiting with perfection.

1 ... 2 ... 3, echoing in my mind as the ball would hit the floor with every dribble. Nothing else existed as the soft fluid of electricity began intensifying in my stomcak. It rose from behind my navel and into my heart – *Serenity.*

Euphoria began to fill my head as the soothing waters of peace calmed every stress, every worry, o*h my God, I love this game.* Shot, after shot, after shot, it seemed as if time didn't exist. I was lost in the feeling of peace as I watched my body from within my mind go through the motions of the shot. Like an observer, sitting in the center of a lake, watching all life go on around him. I sat at the center of my mind as a silent watcher, witnessing everything, and investing in none.

My body continued on with its motions, shooting an orange looking sphere into a round piece of hard shiny substance. My lungs burning with the fire of the intense drive that was motivating my actions. Yet I was at a distance, almost confused as to what my body

63

was doing with the orange sphere. Deeper and deeper, I was moving into the ocean of my consciousness, and with every level of depth, the outside world faded more and more out of my awareness, until there was nothing. No movement, no thought, no witnessing my body go through strange motions, just stillness.

Floating in a vast nothingness, no light and no dark, my mind registered no thing, no fluctuation of my mind except the feeling of being connected to every part of this vastness. I was whole. There was no separation or confusion. I felt every part of me unify with every thing, and in turn, to no thing. I was transported to a place where there was no existence of anything except this vast nothingness, which felt like every thing. And I was every part of it, *I AM whole.*

The sense of time had become irrelevant. It felt as if I had been *existing in* that state for an *eternity.* I could neither grasp the beginning nor the end of anything, there was no beginning or end to grasp, just a feeling of eternity.

What is this place? Immediately, as the question surfaced, I began to see mirage-like images flickering on and off in the distance. "What's going on?" I said to myself.

As soon as I said that, the voice began echoing throughout this space, and with every echo the mirage-like images began to intensify with color. Still unable to make anything out, *am I doing this, am I creating these things?*

Instantly, these images, flashing with intense brilliance, started coalescing as puzzle pieces coming together. One by one, the pieces would snap in, flash and unite with the rest of the image, erasing the lines distinguishing it as an individual piece.

What is this … what's happening? Thoughts began racing through my head. With an explosion, the pieces began connecting at hyper-speed until eventually I could make out what looked like a gym.

Continuing to coalesce, the image started moving towards me taking on three-dimensional depth. As it was moving closer towards me, I could see that it was the gym that I had previously been in. With a final surge of movement in my direction, the image engulfed everywhere around me, yet it was still a translucent, mirage-like, holographic projection. As the image came to a halt, it felt like I was accelerating at light speed, and a moment later, the acceleration faded as my head dropped and my eyes opened.

"What the fuck!" I said in astonishment. Now staring down at the basketball between my legs, I could see I was sitting on the floor, leaning against the wall just underneath the basket. Looking up, the expanse of the gym in front of me, my forearms resting on my bent knees, and my fingers clenched around each other just tight enough to keep my arms from falling off my knees.

Bewildered, I began searching my mind to try and remember how I got in this position. After a few seconds to no avail, *I know I was standing at the free-throw line, but how the hell did I get here … and what the fuck was all that?*

"Free-will deconstructs the solidarity of your context," a voice shot through my awareness.

Free-will deconstructs context … what the hell does that mean? "Free-will deconstructs the solidarity," *of my context … my context.* Memories of my life began flashing in my mind. I sat there watching the movie of my life become a fluid-like screen. As I watched everything of my past, my context, my frame of reference, turn into a swirling ocean of colors, and immediately it all made sense.

My past is my past, I don't live there, I live now … in the Now … guided by free-will … by infinite possibility. My context appears to solidify only when I assume my past reality determines my future actions … it doesn't though … I exist now, not then, 'then' is only a memory, not a reality. Now is the only reality, and now is guided by the infinite possibility of free-will … the freedom to be who I AM, right now.

As those words consciously moved through my thought process, a light flashed in my mind and my body was overcome with that same soft, fluid electricity, vibrating with ripples of intensity, and softly crashing waves of stillness.

It was the most orgasmic feeling I had ever felt, and it was all because I could feel my paradigm about the true meaning of life expand into a realm of thought I had only ever read about. Like all the sages and prophets of old, all blessed me, all at once with their divine wisdom. And I only saw the cover of the book that they had once written with their lives.

Now I'm sitting there, staring at the book of life and it's a story of my life. The book of life and its meaning instantly jumped into my conscious-awareness, and was there only for a fleeting moment. All I could see was the cover, and the cover was a picture of my life. *I wonder if that's how it is for everybody?*

Not knowing what to do, I looked over to my left and saw Wallace, my brother from another mother, and daddy too. Seeing him shook my mind free of the previous moment. He was sitting on the ground doing his cool-down stretches from his workout with the track team.

It felt good to see a familiar face, *especially after everything I have gone through today*. Everything I was experiencing up to this point had felt positive, but I still had this un-easy feeling about it all.

I don't fucking like thinkin I might be clinically insane, but whatever. Wallace was still finishing up his stretch routine as my mind began to wander through memories of how Wallace and I first met.

I'm not even sure of all the specifics of how Wallace and I even met. S*hit, when we actually started chillin for real,* but like Lavont, it felt like he was a soul-brother to me. *Like, a not of this world brother, like, from another realm type of brother. That's how it feels* when I met all my good friends, like we were meant to meet up in this life, like we have a similar mission to accomplish. *Like we was sent down here and our destiny is tied together somehow.*

That's how I have felt with my real brothers, so I just started seeing my friends as my family, showed the same respect, and it wasn't long before we expressed that family type of love to one another.

Damn, the first time I met Lavont, that was my first day on campus just back from Annual Training to be an Ammunition Supply Specialist for my Reserve Unit. I'll never forget that day, standing there while this black guy with dreads, took the initiative to come introduce himself to a white guy's, and shake his hand in genuine interest, *not that bullshit 'playin nice' just for looks.* And from that day forward I knew the philosophy of racism was invalid and irrational, *one race superior than another, that's straight bullshit.*

"Ay, wut up cuz?" My mind snapped back to the gym as Wallace reached in to greet with the usual dap. "Wut it do," he asked with his soft spoken mentality.

"Not much man," I replied, speaking as calmly as he had asked. "I'm just havin a crazy-ass day, so I thought I'd shoot."

"Ay, you wunna get down on some horse?" Wallace asked.

"Yeah, I 'spose I could do that. I still owe ya a lesson from last time. I never got to finish givin ya yo education on big-man moves," I said with a smirk, now waiting for his usual sarcastic wit-filled comeback.

Looking at me like he didn't even want to start cracking jokes, he said, "Nah bro, I'm jus here to get my title back. Ya know how it is, a nigga gotta get wut's rightfully his. Can't let no white man keep me down." As he said that, he looked at me with a half smile on his mouth and laughter in his eyes.

"Aight, dat's wut's up," I said. "Hey, you know it's not cuz I hate your skin color that I have to win all the time. It's just that I, I know you learn somethin every time you see me play. And I feel like I'm cheatin ya in a way by not showin you everything I got."

"Yeah, that's cool bro, I know that," Wallace said while walking towards the free-throw line. "Dat's the thing 'bout bein alive bro, it's yo heaven or ya hell, you can reveal whateva the hell ya want, from now n into tha everlivin existence of God, or Allah if ya prefer, or maybe ya call it The Universe, or Jah," he said, raising his arm to point at me. "Ya, that's it, your's is Jah."

I stopped tying my shoe as I watched him stand at the free throw line waiting for me to throw him the ball. *Jah, what the fuck is Jah? … I need to look that shit up later … cuz right now, I need to whip some ass in this game they call horse.*

I snatched the ball that was off to my left and turned to throw it to him as he was going through the motions of his shot. "Here ya go bro," I said while gently dropping the ball to roll it to him. "Ya need to warm up or anything?" I asked as he waited patiently for the ball.

As the ball reached his feet, he slowly scooped down to pick it up. Starting to dribble, he said, "Nah nigga, I'm good, I don't need to warm up for ya to catch dis beat down. I'm gonna take it nice n slow to let you see a real lesson in this game dey call hawse."

What was that, he just said the exact phrase I just thought? ... Fuck it, whatever.

He stood there, eyeing the rim in his lazy-like posture, his hips began to move, and with a whisper, the ball fell through with the net moving only slightly.

Wallace had always perplexed me. He was the first guy I had ever met that was more mysterious than I had ever known myself to be. I think that is what initially intrigued me about him. Most anybody else, I would have an intuitive feeling that I already had them figured out, and it would usually happen within the first few conversations we had. Wallace though, he was a mystery I had never before seen.

He was every thing that I wanted to be – self-assured, a lady's man, handsome, intelligent and with a down-to-earth wisdom. He was also everything I disliked – arrogant, manipulative, vain, smart-ass, and with a know-it-all attitude.

What I can't understand, is how this man can have the characteristics that I aspire to, yet he still displays the pretense I despise.

"Well, that's just because you see both sides of the same coin," a voice-like thought bubbled up from the back of my head. *"For every yin there is a yang ... for every up there is a down ... and for everything that you perceive as good ... you will also see what you consider as bad, and once you remove ... from your mind ... the need for duality to exist ... you will*

then see that you must risk looking like everything you hate ... in order to be everything that you seek ... It is as the Mahatma Gandhi once said ... you must be the change you seek."

Standing there, with my head cocked, staring at the rim in a half-daze as Wallace's shot bounced off the near side of the rim towards me. Reaching up with my left hand, I snatched the ball, pivoting to the lower block, moving into a post position on the right side of the hoop.

"Entry pass," I said, spinning the ball out in front of me, grabbing it as it bounced back up at me. "Fake left," twitching my left shoulder. "Power dribble right, into the center of the lane ... baby-hook-left," I whispered just loud enough for him to hear me as I stared up towards the front of the rim, watching my left hand flick the ball in. Landing solid and standing strong, with my arm still in the follow-through position, "Ya know, cuz you gotta be able to go both ways. Both the right, and the left," I said still standing in the same position.

Grabbing the ball bouncing beneath the hoop, Wallace, whispering to himself, said, "Fuckin left." Lightly shaking his head in disbelief, he moved to the same position I had just started from. Watching him as I backed out of the way, up to the top of the key, he spun the ball out in front of him, grabbed it, faked left, power-dribbled right finishing with a baby hook. His left hand bounced softly as the ball sailed through the opening of the rim.

"That's aight tho, cuz I'm like tha yin ta yo yan," he said, jawing back to me as he landed, still mimicking me. "I'm like erything you wanna be, and erything at'cha already are."

Aight now, that's kinda creepy. He just said the same shit I thought, again. "Hey Wallace, what you know 'bout telepathy," I asked, slightly laughing. I picked the ball up as it bounced back to me at the free-throw line.

"Telepathy? Not much, why?"

"Ah, just cuz you keep readin my thoughts and it's kinda creepy," I said going through my free-throw routine. "Fuckin Charles, get ya head out my mind. *I'M THE JUGGERNAUT BITCH!* Yo weapons cannot harm me. Don't chu know who I AM." Looking at him as he stood off to the left, quietly waiting for me to finish my shot, I took the shot never looking at the rim, a moment later I heard the net splash. "Pimp-smack yo ass bitch … ya my hooka now," I said, still standing in the release of my shot.

Waiting a few seconds, he then took a few steps towards the ball as it bounced back towards the free throw line. "I want it, I want it willingly," he said with a shrill voice as he stepped in front of me. "Ay, dat reminds me, I got some hoes comin up from Omaha t'night," he said as I moved over to the right side of key, free-throw line extended. "We can get fucked up like last night, still got liquor n green, we jus need blunt wraps n juice."

"Yah, I don't see why not," I said. "That actually reminds me, I got this prospect on the line, and she's talkin that she wants a black guy. If I can get it worked out, are ya down?"

"How much?" he asked.

"I don't know yet, just started talkin to her. She's older though, like forty somethin, but she said she was down, so it is what it is I guess. I'll keep talkin to her bout it."

Facing Revelation

Wallace never broke rhythm as he finished his free-throw routine. Pausing before he took his shot, he turned only his head towards me but continued to stare at the rim out the corner of his eyes, and while shooting, he said, "Ay you know me, I don't discriminate, a ho is a ho. Just get at me when she wants it."

The net snapped as the ball sank through, splashing it upwards wrapping around the front of the rim. Jogging into the lane, I grabbed the ball and moved back to the free-throw line saying, "What can I say, I get fuckin hacked, I got two shots at the line this time." Reaching the free-throw line, I turned and positioned myself for my second shot. "Oh hey, before I forget, I'm not gonna stay up too late tonight, I got drill tomorrow and gotta be in Lincoln by seven a.m."

"Damn cuz, when you gonna be done with that Army Reserve shit?" he asked with concern in his voice.

"I don't know, I got a while before my time's up. I'm in a Drill Sergeant unit now though, so it's all good. Chances of me goin to Iraq are pretty slim. Like I can even get there anyway, I've been alerted twice now, and sent home both times before gettin to the mobilization station."

"You actually want to go?" he asked. "You know that's a bullshit war right? Fuck, what war isn't?" he said with a disgusted tone.

"Hey man, I don't really know what the deal is, so if I got a job to do, I ain't got no reason why I can say no. Ya feel me?"

"I feel ya. What the hell d'you join for anyway, you don't seem like the fightin type?"

"College money bro, college money. But then I found that there other parts I like. There are parts I don't, but I can deal with that," I said while continuing to dribble beyond my usual three dribbles. "You know that's the trap they use now days. Charge an ass-load for college, then tell the majority of the people, the people who can't afford college, that they'll get all this money for college for joinin, then when it comes to payin up, ya got ten miles of red tape to go through. Fuckin, last semester they shorted me my tuition assistance. But hey, it's whatever, I signed the contract, so, it is what it is. But more than that, when we actually do something, I like it. I could easily see myself making a career out of it, but I'd def have to get into some kind of action to make it worth my time."

Still dribbling, I lost myself in a train of thought chugging through my memories. No longer concerned about what I was doing, I put up a half-ass shot and watched as it banked short off the front of the rim.

Chapter 5 - Drill

God I fuckin hate drill, I thought as the alarm clock on the dresser continued screaming. *When am I gonna be done with this shit?* Jumping up from the bed, slamming my fist on the clock, a piece of plastic splintered off. I began the customary procedures of getting dressed in my costume for the weekend. Opening the closet door, the all-too-familiar green, black, and brown Battle Dress Uniform hung next to the green pickle-suit more appropriately dubbed the Class A Uniform.

This is bullshit, wake up at o'dark thirty in the morning "to go sit my ass at drill and do absolutely nothing but look at the fuckin wall," I whispered to myself. *Just stay here, call in, say your car broke down ... or no, better yet, tell 'em it has a flat ... maybe I'll get a flat on the way in and I'll have a real reason ... only if you're lucky.*

Continuing to don my outfit, the costume I would put on once a month to go play Army Man, *man, I wish I could go back to sleep,* my mind drudged through the forecast of what my day was going to look like. *Sitting around, sitting around, sitting around,* I thought as my mind played back memories of the countless hours I've spent literally watching time click off the clock while at drill. *Oh hey we can go to lunch,* "a free meal, the only part worth getting out of bed for." *Sitting around, sitting around, sitting around, when the fuck are we gonna get outta here, sitting around, sitting around, sitting around, DISMISSED, oh yeah, and be here tomorrow for another day of Jack-Shit!*

As I stood up to walk out the door, I glanced in the mirror to ensure my uniform was properly donned, and to see if my rank was still in alignment from last month. In the previous four years in the military, since being done with Basic Training, I think I had washed my uniform two or three times. It never got dirty unless we went out to the field and actually played in the dirt, and that had only happened once.

The rest of the time was spent sitting around at the Unit, doing nothing. Maybe performing preventative maintenance checks and services on the vehicles or other equipment, but that would be a highlight of the day, something to look forward to.

It didn't take long for me to lose myself in thought on the hour and a half drive I had to actually get to drill, *oh wait no, it's called Battle Assembly now … we have to be all professional and shit.* I always love watching the commercials on TV that glamorize being a Citizen Soldier, *they never tell ya about the boring shit.*

Time seemed to drift as I was lost in thought, it was now about ten till seven, almost time for our first formation. I pulled into the parking lot, parked and made my way inside and up to our company area. *Time to put the game face on.*

"Morning Specialist," I heard from behind as I rounded the corner into the company assembly area.

Turning to see who had greeted me, I saw the sawed-off shotgun standing there before me that was my Command Sergeants Major. Immediately snapping to parade rest and up against the wall, "Morning Sergeants Major," I responded with respect.

"I need to see you later. DON'T forget," he ordered as he marched in front of me, pausing for a moment, his head tilting upward, his eyes catching mine a foot above his. Rolling his eyes with a smile, he continued on into his office.

I continued to stand against the wall as I watched him walk away. *What the fuck is this all about, what the fuck did I do?*

"Hey Morris, what was that all about," came the voice of my Section Sergeant, Sergeant First Class Caldrich.

"I don't know Sarn't, I just got here," I said, still standing with my feet shoulder width apart, hands clasped behind me in the small of my back in the "At Ease" position. "I swear I didn't do anything wrong, I swear on the U.S. Army," I said half laughing as I put my hand over the nametape with the words U.S. Army.

"FORMATION," a deep voice bellowed from down the hall.

Here we go, the fun's begun. "Who's got the guide-on?" I asked, stepping into the First Sergeants office to grab the company flag.

"Somebody's already has it downstairs," I heard from outside the office.

Making my way downstairs and into the lunchroom that also serves as the formation area, I took my beret from my pocket and began the intricate process of donning it. *I can't wait till I get done with Drill Sergeant's school and I can wear that hat,* I thought while looking at the twenty or so Drill Sergeants with the Smokey the Bear style brown covers on their heads. *That shit's a hell of a lot easier to put on than this fuckin thing.*

The next forty-five minutes seemed to drag on as we went through the motions of the weekend's first formation. It became interesting for about ten minutes near the end when Sergeants Major Murphy began playing his fatherly role, while giving his wisdom of conducting ourselves in a professional manner while in our civilian lives, "As all your actions bear significance upon the totality of all areas of your life," he said with stern authority.

"You cannot think you play two separate games, one as a civilian and one as a soldier. You must conduct yourself with utmost regard for the uniform you wear, and everything it represents. Men and women have died serving in the uniform you now wear. Serving the nobility of freedom for all. With that being said, I DO NOT want any more reports on my desk, of soldiers, not holding themselves to the standards upon which you have sworn an oath to uphold. YOU signed the contract, I WILL, hold you to it."

This guy can't know I smoke weed, I know for damn sure my name ain't on no damn report … FUCK! this it too close. The thoughts continued as I remained steadfast at "Parade Rest." As my thoughts continued, his words became an inaudible hum my conscious mind couldn't make out. I was too engrossed in all the ways I was **not** holding myself to the standard Sergeants Major Murphy was just referring to. And in the pit of my stomach was a knot of guilt, because I knew he was right.

Swallowing the war of good vs. evil that ensued in my gut, I clenched my teeth a little harder and focused my attention back on CSM Murphy.

"BATTALION!" he barked, standing centered on the formation about seven feet withdrawn in front of the battalion.

Immediately, all the First Sergeants in front of each company formation snapped to the position of attention. "COMPANY!" they echoed CSM Murphy's preparatory command, while looking over their right shoulders.

"Atennn-TION," CSM Murphy ordered.

A moment later, all the men and women in the room were standing at attention, awaiting the next command.

"FIRST Sergeants, take command of your companies, conduct your daily duties." Pausing for a moment, then taking a step with his left foot, across his body, in the usual manner of exiting a formation from that position, he walked straight until he reached the door where he stopped at the podium to collect his paperwork.

The First Sergeants took a step forward, did an about face, and we began our day. Standing mindlessly at the back of the group, starring at the shine on the toe of my boot, my mind and gut were still engulfed in the internal conflict brought about by the words of CSM Murphy.

We finished our brief company meeting. I made my way to my usual spot up in the classroom, *for yet another mind wandering class* on some basic soldier skill I learned back in Basic Training. *This is ridiculous, how many times do we have to go through this shit.*

Reaching the door to the classroom, I heard the familiar voice of CSM Murphy bellow from behind me. "Specialist Morris," I turned to look and immediately went to parade rest, "are you doing anything important right now?"

"No Sarn'ts Major," I replied.

"My office. Now."

I took to feet and lengthened my stride to catch up to him. Making our way through the maze of office cubicles, we reached his office. He stepped off to the right of his door and extended his right arm to usher me into his office. Sitting in a chair across his, he entered and began filing the papers in his hand.

"So Specialist, how are you doing?"

What the fuck am I suppose to say, "I'm good Sarn'ts Major, just takin it one day at a time."

"That's good to hear," he said as he finished with the papers. He grabbed the back of his chair and sat down. "What are doing a month from now," he asked. Continuing on without waiting for an answer, he said, "We need someone to represent the battalion at the brigade Soldier of the Year competition and you seem to conduct yourself with the appropriate level of professionalism to represent us. Plus, your brother went for us two years ago and did okay, and he said you might like to try it."

A small smile creased across my lips as I internally laughed at the irony of the situation. "Uhm, I would be happy to Sarn'ts Major." *This is funny, they have no idea, and now they want me to represent them … well that's just cuz I'm the shit, I'm smooth like that … yeah, that's it,* I thought to myself, full of sarcasm. *Shut the fuck up and be quiet, they don't know shit, and this will help to get you in good. Just fuckin do it. And stop FUCKING smoking.*

"I'll fill you in on the details later, Specialist. Do you have any questions?"

"When do I get my orders Sarn'ts Major?"

"We'll get those this week and email 'em to you so you can print 'em off. In the meantime, get some manuals on basic soldier skills."

"I will Sarn'ts Major."

"Oh, and Specialist, don't do anything stupid. This can look good on your résumé. And if you win, I'll let you go to active duty Drill Sergeants School. Last time we talked, that's what you wanted, correct?"

"Yes, Sergeants Major."

"Good, now get out of my office," he said as he smiled a sly smile. Rising from his chair, he opened the door for me to exit. As he did, a line of First Sergeants, with papers and file folders in hand, waited for me to exit so they could see him.

That's right bitches, you wait for me, a Specialist. Hahahaha, fuckers ... dude, seriously, shut the fuck up.

The rest of the day was no different than any other Battle Assembly, and after being dismissed, I jumped in my navy blue, big body 1984 Fleetwood Brougham Cadillac, and made my way to Shanelle's house.

Chapter 6 – Tha Biznass

Arriving at Shanelle's apartment complex, I made my way through the winding maze of mediocrity, one apartment building after another would move out from around the bend as I continued. The sprawling growth of modern suburbia was accented by the groaning sounds of the many bulldozers, excavators and dump trucks paving the earth, making way for yet one more building. To house contemporary society's latest manifestations, *and the human pukes who can't seem to control their own over-consumption.*

Just as I, *whoa, whoa, whoa dude,* reached her building, another car was backing out of the parking stall. *Settle down. Human pukes? Seriously, take it easy.* Waiting for the car to fully exit the space and move on, my mind flashed with a memory of the day before sitting with professor Filler as we neared the end of our discussion. "Forgiveness, you might try it sometime," he said, as if the memory was as real as it was yesterday. *What, what the h…*

Releasing the pressure on the brake, the car slowly inched forward *what the hell was that?* Goosing the accelerator, the big body surged forward as I cranked the wheel to the right, *whatever,* gliding into the parking stall.

"Fuckin perfect," I said with a conceited grin, *as usual, I can't help it,* "Perfection is my nature."

Yo, you conceited asshole, "shut the fuck up, seriously," saying to myself, laughing at the ridiculousness of my own pathetic attempt at looking cool for nobody except the image of me in my own mind.

"Forgiveness," the memory of professor Filler resurfaced. This time, I could almost hear the words as an audible voice outside my mind.

Gathering my bags in the passenger seat with my right hand, while opening the door with my left, the door abruptly stopped as it thudded against the red Dodge Durango in the stall next to me. *Whoops! Fucked that up.* I inched the door off the side panel of the Durango, squeezed the handles of my bags, and slid myself sideways, out the cracked open door. *One thing at a time Mike.*

I wonder what she's got for me this time, I thought to myself, visualizing all the cool shit Shanelle could have bought me as I made my way to the front door. *"Hey, you know if you keep goin the way you are, you're gonna have to up your rates to more than just clothes and shoes and shit."*

Making my way to the front door of the building, and pressing the square, black plastic button labeled 303. Seconds later a buzz. Then a pop, as the lock unlatched releasing the door's seal. Opening the door, I quickly made my way up the three flights of stairs. Reaching the top, another door stood between me and the hallway leading to Shanelle's apartment. Not breaking stride, I moved with swiftness through the door and down the hallway trying to get to her door before she would expect me to be there.

Reaching to knock, the door cracked opened before my knuckles hit the wood of the door. Slowly pushing the door open and stepping in, "Honey, I'm home!" I shouted as I threw my bags down, opening my arms for a hug.

Slowly, the timid eyes appeared from behind the door followed by a giant smile. "I missed you Michael."

"Yeah? I missed you too."

"You're gonna have to come around more often, I get too lonely when I don't see you," Shanelle said as she laid her head against my heart, poking her arms between my ribs and arms, wrapping me in warmth.

Cupping her head with my right hand and holding her against me with my left, we stood holding each other, embracing in a tender love. Just standing, we held tight to each other for a brief eternity.

Peeling her head off my chest, she craned her neck back, still holding on to me, she pinned her chin against my sternum. Gazing into the blue oceans, I was taken by the depth her eyes conveyed. Her pupils opened wide as she spoke, "I don't know what it is about you, but I love hugging you. I feel engulfed when you hold me. In a good way." Squeezing me tighter, "I can't get enough of you Michael."

Whoa this bitch is crazy, "I can't get enough of you either," I said squeezing her just a little tighter, giving my best act. *I barely see her and already she's addicted to the dick, she needs to get laid by someone other than me.*

"You're not like other guys I've met, you actually care," she said.

That's what you think… dude, seriously? You're an asshole sometimes, "I like to listen, it's a good way to get to know somebody. To actually listen for once."

"I think that's what makes me attracted to you, you're about more than just 'gettin some,' like most guys."

"Yeah, well, I do what I can. Even if I don't like a person, I have to listen to 'em to understand 'em. A human is like any other system. You have to listen to it to assess its requirements." I said while letting her go, raising my hands to her shoulders, I arched back, extended my arms, and lowered my chin to my chest to get a more level perspective to look into her eyes. "So how've you been since the last time I saw you?"

"Good, just workin," she said, looking away in a timid glance to the ground.

"Nah, now-now, what's with the uncertainty. What's really goin on inside there," I said, tapping her heart with my finger.

"Oh nothing." Letting go of me she turned to walk away and into her room.

"Now hold on a sec Shanelle," softly speaking to her. "You said I care. I said I listen. The only way I can listen and know what to care about is if you let me know what's havin you be sad."

Stopping at her bed, she turned, looked at me, then down to the ground and sat on the edge of her bed. Still looking at the ground, obviously dejected, she began to speak, "I feel like nobody wants me in this world, you're the only person I can talk to on a real level. And you only come around when you have drill and need a place to stay." Looking up at me, I could see her eyes glisten as tears began to form. "I mean, I know our relationship is more of a business nature, but I just don't want to feel so lonely anymore. I just want somebody to lay next to me at night, you know. Somebody to come home to. Somebody to think about. Somebody to talk to about love. Somebody to care about." Still looking into my eyes, she uttered, "Do you understand what I'm saying?"

Fuck! ... fuckin drama... wait... take a breath and be here for her, I thought as I stood in the doorway leaning against the door jam. She looked again towards the ground as I spoke, "Look Shanelle, life is life, it happens. We're born alone and we'll die alone. The best we can do is have fun while were here. Forget what the world wants of you, all that shit is what it is. We're individuals with a power to choose, YOU can CHOOSE to be happy or YOU can CHOOSE to be like this.

"You're situation is what you make it." Shanelle kept her gaze at the floor, her body showing dejection. "Shanelle, look at me. I'm here to be honest. Honesty is what makes me the guy you can talk to. So just know that everything I say is to help you be a better you. I mean no disrespect, I simply have to speak from what I see. Otherwise I'm lying, and it feels like shit to lie, and it doesn't benefit the relationship in any way."

Stopping for a moment to collect my thoughts, I took a deep breath, then continued on. "Whether you're lonely or not doesn't make a difference. That's an external condition, you must be whole within yourself if you ever wanna have the chance to not feel lonely. Loneliness is a state of mind, it's an idea, we must let go of the ideas in order to recognize the truth that we're all connected anyway. And the more we clear our energy fields from the BS, the more we tune into the happiness that is the essence of who we are."

Moving over to the bed, I cupped my right hand under her chin and softly began to lift. Her head tilted back. As her head rose, I bent over at the waist, reaching with my left hand and grabbing her shoulder. Looking into her eyes and smiling. Purposely smiling as big as I could, I spoke softly to her, "Don't worry, BE happy."

Still looking into her eyes, my face inches from hers, her eyes began to melt with a flicker of her eyelids, she began to stand, and as she rose, our lips met with a moist caress. Entwining our arms around one another, our lips remained in the embrace of tender solace, freezing in a moment of forever, and just for that instant, we held each other tight, not moving.

As the warmth of her body radiated the fragrance of the blooming of spring time, my groin began to pulsate with cataclysms of ecstasy. Squatting down to her, I squeezed her tighter and lifted her into my arms. Moving a step closer to the bed, bending over in slow passion, I laid her softly upon the bed. Our lips never breaking the seal of tenderness.

Now on top of her, pressing my hips against hers, reaching beneath her back with my left arm and squeezing her tight to me once more, all of her body against mine – lips still locked, tongues now furiously searching the depths of each other's mouth.

I love you, I said in my mind as I visualized a beam of light from my heart to hers. With a quick breath, she squeezed me tighter. Now more tenderly, she caressed my upper lip with her tongue. A wave of tingles began to rainbow through my lip. She continued to caress my lips softly. A pulse of intense heat flamed up from my groin. Pressing my hips to hers, I began to visualize a flame extend from my groin to hers. As I continued, slowly, I began to move my hips in circles. Ensuring my organs of ecstasy were caressing hers.

Releasing our lips I moved my cheek to hers and whispered into her ear, "Everything's gonna be alright." Inhaling the sweet fragrance of her hair, I pressed my cheek to hers with softness, lightly licking the crevasses of her ear. Reaching my left hand around the nape of her neck, I held her head with my right, still slowly inhaling. Feeling warmth in my chest, I showered her with that glowing warmth. I spoke again in whispers, "Just be here now."

Continuing to taste her flesh, I softly moved my tongue from her ear, to her neck, to her shoulder, down to her throat, and up to her chin, and up to her bottom lip. Sucking her bottom lip into my mouth, I tenderly bit and began to caress it with my tongue.

With a soft moan, she became weak in my arms as she surged her hips upwards. Moving her arms below my lower back, she pulled my hips into hers as she opened her legs allowing more contact.

Still separated between layers of clothes, my organs pulsating with pleasure, I began to glide my hips up and down, firmly pressing the pinnacle of my excitation into the moistness of her jubilation.

"Uhhh!" she groaned as she arched her back causing us to break our lips apart. She began to softly moan, "Mmhhh," as I continued to undulate my hips. "I want you now," she whispered as she opened her eyes, looking into mine.

"Not yet," I whispered back, "Patience begets the wonders of ecstasy."

Undoing the buttons that barely contained her breasts beneath, I took off her shirt. As I unhooked her bra, she reached and undid my belt and began to unbutton my trousers. Pulling the bra upward, her arms rose above her head. I took both of them with my left hand and pinned her wrists together above her head.

Now laying to the side of her I cleared the hair away from her neck as I began to softly explore side of her neck with my tongue. At the same time, reaching with my right fingertips to her pubic mound and softly pressing with four fingers.

Feeling her quiver, I released the pressure and began to softly caress her stomach with a slow figure eight. Moving my tongue to the side of her breast, near her nipple, I teased, just on the skirts of her areola. Circling around in slow, soft moistness.

Still clasping her wrists with my left, I reached with my right to her head, turning her head while raising my lips to hers – embracing with gentleness. Reaching my right hand down, I began to unbutton her pants. Slowly unzipping her pants, I parted the flaps. Reaching between her soft satin panties and jeans, down to the treasure of her femininity. The moistness assured me she was enjoying herself.

Our lips still embracing with gentleness, I removed my hand and began to slowly remove her jeans. Releasing her wrists, she moved her arms down to help in the removal of her pants.

We removed her pants and then her panties, she moved up to the head of her bed, "Come here," she said alluring me with the taunt of her finger.

"Hold on, I gotta take off my boots," I said, taking a seat on the edge of the bed.

As I sat down, I felt the bed move as she crawled up behind me; she reached around to unbutton my shirt. Getting one boot undone I kicked it to the side as she pulled my shirt off, she then started on my undershirt. Before I could get the other boot undone, she began to lift the shirt off. I sat up, she took it the rest of the way off. I leaned back over to finish the boot as she caressed my back.

"I love your tattoo," she said as she leaned in and began to softly kiss my back.

Finishing with the boot I kicked it to the side, stood up and turned around to face her. She sat there, kneeling on the bed in glowing radiance with a gentle smile. She reached to me and finished the buttons on my trousers that she didn't get the first time. Opening my pants up, they slid down to the floor.

"I forgot you don't wear underwear," she said.

"Yeah, it stifles my boys, and I can't have that now can I?" She smiled at me, then moved to the head of the bead, alluring me with the taunt of her finger. I crawled onto the bed and up to her. Me straddling over top of her, our lips embraced once more. Moving my right hand down to her inner thigh, softly stroking her warm flesh I began to venture near the heart of her ecstasy. Moving ever closer with each stroke, ensuring not to touch.

She opened her legs wider; I moved my hand to her stomach to keep her guessing in anticipation. Now stroking downward, ever closer with each stroke. Moving my hands through the trimmed bristles upon the top of her feminine mound. I softly pulled. Then quickly slid my fingers down over the hood of her desire to the moist evidence of her femininity, and back up again to the bristles.

With a slow softness, I moved my hand again to her other inner thigh and began stroking. Working ever closer to her orgasmic treasure.

Releasing my lips from hers, I ventured with my tongue down through the valley of her neck, up to the stiff summit of her breasts. Softly biting and flicking her nipple with my tongue, she clenched my back with the sharpness of her fingernails.

The fingers of my right hand now slowly circled the opening to her bliss, the tip of my index finger venturing a peek into the temple of her sacred sexuality. Slowly extending the tip in, she began to moan with pleasure in her voice. The walls of her temple pulsated tightly around as my finger ventured ever deeper. Reaching the Great-spot. The pyramid of her delight. I pressed.

"oohhhh!" she moaned as her back arched. Her hips rose and her legs quivered with vibrations of certain pleasure.

I began to quickly move my finger back and forth over the pyramid. She began to writhe.

Removing my tongue from her nipple, I positioned myself, now kneeling, looking at the door to her temple. She continued to wiggle as my finger continued to caress.

"Oh my god, what are you doing to me," she cried out.

"Whatever I want," I said as I removed my finger, looking up to her eyes, *I own you bitch... and I'll do whateva the hell I want... dude, you are seriously fucked in the head. Be present with her.*

She continued to lay, quietly staring at me with a soft smile. "I want you to take me now," she said with soft sincerity.

Crawling over top of her once more, I leaned in next to her ear and quietly said with a deep voice, "You're wish is my command."

Thinking of the condom in my bag, *nah, you don't need it, you have control*, I thought to myself. *And it's not like she's with anybody else, you own her.*

"Do you have a condom?" she said.

"Nah, I don't have cooties if you don't."

"I don't, but what about, well, you know?"

"Don't worry 'bout that, I got that under control," I said as I reached down to introduce my now erect guru, into her, now prepared temple of sacred sexuality.

Facing Revelation

Chapter 7 – Division Soldier of the Year

Standing at the front of the room full of Sergeants Majors, Generals, Colonels, and all sorts of high ranking personnel, my mind was focused on breathing calmly and holding the position of attention.

Through a haze of moments, I then found myself sitting at a table towards the back of the room holding a handful of unit coins given to me by an array of high ranking officers and NCO's. Sitting with the familiar faces of people from my unit. Both cherishing and despising the lime light, a feeling of anxious excitement continued to reverberate in my stomach.

Over the past 9 months, since the Battle Assembly I found out I was competing for Brigade Soldier of the Year, I had stopped smoking and drinking. I again started working out. I read several of the manuals to prepare. And I also started meditating on a daily basis. But in general, I still felt largely unprepared.

Now that I stood in front of a room full of highly respected individuals as one who had earned respect, a sense of integrity arose in my body. I sensed a resurgence of honoring a value system. That same feeling that had been so powerful in Basic Training. Of believing in myself. And of acting honestly.

What I didn't know was that my world was about to change. It had been several weeks since CSM Murphy told me I could take my military career in any direction. And active duty Drill Sergeant School was a thrilling opportunity to contemplate. Followed by a Warrant Officer as helicopter pilot.

Knowing that I was already slotted to go, was all the more thrilling. I finally felt I belonged somewhere, and had purpose in a career.

As I arrived back home the night after the ceremony, and sat down to meditate, my mind was drifting in images of the challenges awaiting me at my upcoming training.

My body slowly began to unwind constriction in my muscles. Open relaxation began flowing through the currents of my body's systems. My breath massaged me from the inside out.

I closed my eyelids and focused my eyes up towards the center of my brow. Sensations instantly began to tickle, as a surge of energy shot down from my tailbone. I sensed a connection to the Earth. Then a tenseness in my back, neck, and shoulders began to ache. I began to slowly rotate and stretch each muscle, focusing all of my awareness in each muscle as it was stretched by the rotation of my head.

An unknown number of thoughtless moments passed where the only sensation was expansion. Sensing no separation between myself and the Universe, I felt the edges of all existence.

Moment after moment passed, and all I sensed was connection to everything. Gradually, colors began twirling in my mind's eye. Several swirls later, a picture of a mountain valley with a sunrise cascading its kaleidoscope of colors through the green field. A hawk soared, cutting across the vista.

People began appearing. Each with a smile in the eye. I felt love from each as I looked them in the eye. No words. Only presence in connection to Truth in reality.

As I sat in meditation, my body slumped over. My awareness was lifted, and my body rested. Into what seemed as a dream, my soul flew through the mountain valley as an eagle observing the land. My spirit was at rest.

I woke to find the sun shining into my eyes through the slit created by the separation of a shade away from a window frame. My mind instantly reverted back to the dream of flying as an eagle through the valley of smiling souls. I lay contemplating the possibility of that reality on this planet. As I lay there, I began to see all the impediments to that reality. The darkest and most stark was the reality that millions of children all over the world go to bed hungry every night.

As my mind arose from its slumber in contemplation of a solution to this problem, a friendly thought seemed to appear out of nowhere, *the pen is mightier than the sword*. And instantly, images appeared of writing a blog post on the MySpace account I started. And yet, a toxic feeling of mediocrity filled my stomach.

I thought again of me as an eagle flying through a valley, and I knew that a blog on MySpace was not my destiny. Maybe a stepping stone as a journal of my experience of awakening. But I sensed a depth of something much more significant.

Instantly, my mind was running through reels of Drill Sergeant School. And yet, this too seemed diminished in some way.

Instead of trying to analyze it any further, I pushed it all aside, and decided to go for a walk.

I arrived back at the apartment complex from my walk to the sun shining high on a vast blue sky. I made my way up to mom and dad's apartment. Sat down at the computer to log into my myspace, and socialize. I noticed some emails, some comments, and some interesting looking posts in the site feed.

I checked the emails. I read some comments left on my blog, and made some replies. I navigated back to the main admin area and started perusing the news feed. I saw what amounted to people unhappy with the state of the world and a desire to change things. I began watching videos of the war in Iraq and meandered down that path for several videos. Nothing seemed out of the ordinary. And all was as it should be on a world where domination was the predominant mode of human relationships.

As casual as any other click, my fingers opened a video of the fighting that took place in Fallujah in 2004.

Ten minutes later I was in rage.

Rage was something I hadn't experienced for quite some time. I had learned to suppress it quite well. But as I sat watching, and re-watching a video of children burned alive by what looked like napalm, I was furious.

Furious by the fact that I was associated with an organization that would allow this type of atrocity to occur. Furious that a Commander-in-Chief that I was sworn to obey was condoning these actions. Furious that I was helpless to help these children.

Line after line of possible excuses for such things arose in my mind. But none were substantial to the degree wherein it would justify maiming children.

Fire ignited in my chest. I had to do something. *But WHAT?!* I kept repeating in my mind. *Would I ever carry out such orders if given to me?*

You have brothers who have been there and know the reality of kill or be killed.

I get that, and that's why I question this whole damn thing. If you're telling me that an action to subdue evil, that results in the violation of innocence, is a warranted action to take, YOU HAVE GOT TO BE OUT OF YOUR FUCKING MIND. I don't give a fuck if you call it collateral damage or not. If you violate innocence, you are a coward, and YOU are the evil you say you are fighting.

You have to understand that people will say it's a necessary evil. And if they see it that way, they're gonna believe it.

I don't give a shit what they believe. I say it's Bullshit. So it IS Bullshit. You don't have to agree with me. But trust and believe I'm gonna speak my mind on this issue. I can't just sit here with this in my conscience. Are you fucking kidding me? I mean seriously. If you expect me to sit here knowing that people I ultimately answer to are doing these types of things, and not say anything about it – you're flat ass WRONG.

You have a chain of command, and are only an E-5.

And? I'm a Man with nuts AND A MIND OF MY OWN. I signed that dotted line in testimony of an oath to protect the constitution against both enemies foreign and domestic. And right now, I see the terrorist is the domestic. On my own soil. In anyone who says the action to violate innocence in any way is justified by the necessity of war. You can take your war and stick it up your ass. You tell me to do something like that I'm just gonna stand there and look at you the like the fool you are. You're fucked in the head if you think I'm gonna be part of something like that.

So what are you gonna do?

Tell my chain-of-command precisely what I think, and let them know that I will not be part of an organization that condones the violation of innocence. For the moment, I need to go do some research on the rules of war. Because this is straight up Bull's Shit!

Several hours had passed as he scoured through the rules of War, articles on the Geneva Conventions, and certain UN protocols. He felt a surge of inspiration to write a letter explaining his stance. He recognized it as the same inspiration that moved him to write blog posts.

He opened Microsoft Word and began writing. `"Dear Command Staff..."`[1]

---

[1] See 'Appendix A' for the rest of the letter sent to command.

Chapter 8 – Rally for Peace

"Hey mom," I shouted into the kitchen, "I'm gonna be goin to Lincoln tomorrow, can I use the car?"

"Yeah, I spose', what for, what'r ya doin?"

"Well, there's a peace rally there and I talked to the ones who'r puttin it on, told 'em a little bout what I'm doin with the Army, and asked if they wanted anyone to speak. They said sure, so I guess I'm gonna give a speech."

"Oh, I wish I didn't have to work, I'd like to go."

"Maybe next time," I said as I turned into the kitchen, looking into mom's eyes, smiling while feeling love in my heart.

"What'r ya gonna talk about," mom asked.

"I don't know, peace I guess. Actually, I should probably write somethin huh?"

"Uh, yeah, that might be a good idea."

Turning to the computer, I began contemplating what to say. *What's most appropriate for everyone to hear*, I thought. *I know, the Constitution.*

Google, google... constitution of the United States, I typed into the Google search bar. *Yeah, this feels right, let's start here.* Clicking a link, the page opened, and there it read, We the People of the United States...

Yep yep, I thought, *this is it.* Continuing to coalesce the message that felt most inspiring, I sat at the computer for a few hours until I was completely satisfied it was just right.

Reading through it once as if giving the speech, I felt a surge in my heart, *yep, that's all I need to know.*

I gotta be prepared tomorrow "meditate," I whispered to myself. Looking at the clock it read 9:33 *yeah, meditate for a couple hours, then sleep, wake up, then off to see the wizard.*

Making my way into the spare bedroom, I sat at the head of the bed, brought my legs into lotus pose, looked at Charlie lying next to the bed, then began. "Ayah Asher Ayah," I chanted with a humming whisper initiating the MerKaBa meditation. "Christ Light, Christ Light, Christ Light... Ayah Asher Ayah...Christ Love, Christ Love, Christ Love." Repeating the mantra three times I began to feel energy descend from above, showering over my body.

"Divine Mother Father Creator God of All that Is, I give thanks for all experiences, I ask to be a pure conduit of your Love and Light," I prayed as I moved my fingers into the first mudra.

Continuing through the meditation, and reaching the final prayer, I pursed my lips and blew a puff of wind to initiate the full activation of the light bodies.

Taking a deep breath in, my belly expanded and my chest rose as the lungs filled with air. Reaching full inhale I began to exhale. As I did, my head lowered and my mind drifted into a sleepless state of serenity.

Allowing the intimate bliss of love to continue to infiltrate my beingness, I sat motionless for what seemed like a few minutes. As I began to again feel the physical body, my awareness shifted to the bed beneath me. Continuing to integrate the feeling into the body, I gradually shifted my awareness to my surroundings.

Slowly, I opened my eyes, the room was filled with a soft red glow. Looking around for the origin, I saw the alarm clock sitting on the book shelf just off to his right, *11:11,* I though. *It can't be that late, I was only... shhh ...huh, guess I was in it longer than I thought... oh well, sleepy time.*

"Hey wait," I shouted, "huh, what." Looking at the alarm clock beam 3:33, and seeing it was still dark out. I quickly realized I awoke from a dreamless sleep, "ahh, go to sleep Mike."

A small light crept in through the crack between the shade and window frame. *What, it can't be morning yet, I just went back to sleep.* Rolling over, I turned to see the clock read 7:07 *whatever, I guess I'll get up.*

Making my way to the shower, and looking into the mirror, I raised my arm and turned my head to sniff my armpit, *nah, still fresh as a daisy, I'll save the water for somebody else.*

As the morning drifted from moment to moment, I continued taking actions leading to Lincoln. "There is a... certain set of principles," I bellowed at the steering wheel of the Taurus, pretending I was Martin Luther King. "upon which many people of all ages have lived by and given their lives to secure." *okay dude, you're not really gonna do it like King, so maybe practice like you're gonna do it...*

yeah, I said back to the voice in my head, *well, actually, I don't know how I'm gonna do it, I'll know that when I'm standin there, so can I please just do what I want...*

whatever dude, the voice said back, *just letting you know you look ridiculous drivin down the interstate screamin at the steering wheel like your Martin Luther King...* "yeah, well fuck you too," I said to the steering wheel, imagining it was the other me I was just talkin to in my mind. "You know why 'fuck you'? Cuz it doesn't even matter, that's why... yep, you heard it right, it doesn't even matter."

Looking into the rear view mirror, straight into my own eyes "Dude, look what you're doin to yourself, quit playin that insane game of blame, its not who you are. Really."

A shock of energy buzzed down my spine as I shook my head into a more present embrace of the moment. I leaned back into the seat, noticed a warm feeling in my heart, and watched the roadway move beneath the front of the car.

What seemed like moments later, I found myself coming to a stop light in downtown Lincoln. Winding my way through the maze of one-way streets, I found myself along side the capitol building. Shifting the transmission into park, I noticed an anxious feeling arise in the pit of my stomach.

What d'ya got ta be nervous for, you're just goin to talk to some people. Nothing new dude…breathe.

Closing the door to the car, I started walking towards a group of people gathered at the bottom of the steps leading into the golden domed capitol.

Feeling for the piece of paper in my pocket *dude, relax, everything is all good. Really.* Taking a deep breath, I glanced to the grass to my left, *just be like the grass. Just be.*

"Hi, you here for the rally," an angel in flesh spoke.

"Yeah, I'm Michael, I talked to you on…"

"Yeah, hey, it's so nice to meet you in person," she said. "My name is Melissa. Hey, you wanna sign to hold up."

"Sure, can I hold this one with the peace sign?"

"Yeah, go ahead, my daughter actually made that."

"That's cool, I like that, is this your daughter," I said as I looked to a young one of no more than three years coloring a sign.

"Yeah. Gotta get 'em out here while they're young."

"No doubt, let the children lead the way to peace," I said as I noticed a smile emerge on her face.

"Hey, so we got it set up. I'm gonna say a few things, then introduce you, and then you… you can do your thing."

"That works, just let me know when and where and I'll be there." *This is dope, people gatherin for peace, I can dig this.*

100

The sun shown bright as it began its daily decent to the other side of the planet. I stood watching as countless Beings drove past. Some looking, some looking and honking, some not looking, some driving by with the middle finger in the air. *I wonder if they really know what peace can do for the world*

"Welcome fellow peace lovers," a melodic voice rang out. Turning to look, I saw Melissa standing on the steps with a microphone in one hand and piece of paper in the other. "We're excited to be here today, we love that you came out today to show your support for this cause."

As she spoke, people began to turn from the drone of cars passing by towards this angel of peace uniting them into a stream of focused awareness. "We've got several people here today who'r gonna speak, we've got a soldier who said no to the war, we've got musicians, and we've got you."

Melissa continued introducing the line-up and then entered into her dialogue of why America is in trouble if we allow the atrocities of war to continue. "We cannot allow a group of a few individuals to continue to tear down this country and all is stands for. We've gotta stand up and be heard. WE have to let them know they no longer have free reign to seek out their own agenda. WE are the People. WE say what goes and what stays, and WE have to be the ones to take this country where WE want it to go."

Yo, this chick is dope, definitely came to the right place today. Standing at the bottom of the stage, I continued watching her express her message in passionate tones that rang up my spine.

"And it is my honor to introduce to you a soldier in the 95th division here in Lincoln who, I believe, has a unique message for us all," she said as she turned towards me and extended her arm. "Please welcome Sergeant Michael Morris."

The crowd erupted with cheers as I began walking up the steps to the microphone. *Are these people really cheering for me…whatever, just give your speech.*

I walked to the center of the steps directly in front of the microphone, pulled out the piece of paper the speech was written on, and began my discourse.

Chapter 9 – Nightmares

Hey, what's this, I thought as I passed the doorway. *Women's Locker room*…immediately an arousal began to form deep in the groin. *I wonder if I'll getta see some puss…oh hey, maybe I'll getta stick my dick in it, that'd be even better.*

Walking through the door I began to hear the soft rush of showers being taken. Looking up, a mist billowed over a wall of white square tiles.

Making my way through the maze of lockers, I followed the direction the groin urged me to go. Rounding a corner I saw the entrance as a half toweled woman walked out. *ah, yes, pleasure sweet pleasure…now, before you go in here,* a thought held my focus, *you must commit to having your way with whoever is in here. You cannot hold back in anyway. Take what you want and do what you want, you are free to please yourself…*

Yeah, okay. I agreed with the voice in my mind. Turning the corner into the shower I saw a lonely lady facing the opposite wall. *Oooh, a pudgy one, this oughtta be fun.*

Walkin straight up to the female specimen, I grabbed her shoulder, spun her around and said, "You're gonna have sex with me and there isn't anything you're gonna do to stop me."

"Oh yeah," she said. "what if I wanna have sex with you?"

"Let's do it then."

"No."

"Too bad, you're gettin it anyway." I grabbed her shoulders and pushed her against the wall. Wanting her to bend over I punched her in the stomach, as she leaned forward I thrust my pelvis into her face.

As her face grazed the tip of my penis through my pants. It sent a shockwave through my body. Turning her around, I unzipped my pants, pulled out a full erection and quickly thrust my way into her cavity of fun. *You're mine now bitch...and you're gonna like it...*

*Wait, what the fuck am I doing, this isn't me...*in an instant my eyelids opened to see the bedroom at my parents apartment. *What the fuck was that dream...you're goin insane Mike...just go back to sleep.*

Softly, I began to fall back into the dream state...

Hey, McMikelsen hall, I wonder if Elyssa is around? Continuing to walk up the stairs to the top floor I saw her door was open. Lightly knocking as I walked in, "anybody home?"

"Yeah," she said, "come on in."

"Hey, just stopped into say hi."

"Hi," she said as her lean athletic frame rose from picking up a shirt on the floor. "Hey Mike, do know you're excited" she asked as she looked at my crotch.

"Yeah, that's why I came in to see you, I figured you and I could, you know."

"Okay, that's cool with me."

In a flash of an image I was on top of her, pumping furiously. "ohhh," she moaned as she arched her back and buried her fingernails into my hips.

You like that huh, here, how about this, I said to myself as I jabbed inwards reaching all the way up her cavity to the mound of flesh that I knew to be a Great spot for her pleasure. She instantly squealed as I felt a warm moistness flow out of her and all over my legs. *Yep, I knew you'd like it, you slut.*

I began to thrust faster and faster as I felt a movement of pleasure begin to form and make its way from the bottom of my spine and into the shaft.

Quickly I pulled out and stood up. Holding her on the bed I released a load of pleasure all over her face. She opened her mouth and I quickly thrust it in as more loads kept ejecting. Deep into her throat I moved, she began to push away as she coughed from choking on it. *Na na bitch, you're gettin it all whether you like it or not…*

She looked up, and as our eyes met I could see a helplessness in her. Instantly a sensation of total satisfaction in completely dominating her arose within me, and along with it, a sense of guilt that I was the one doing this to her.

As he began to awake with the sun shining through the window, a consciousness permeated his soul, "Arise Michael, step back and observe your life from a 3rd person perspective. You are more than what consumes you. Be free from it. Objectify the subjectivity of your life. Subjectify the objectivity."

Chapter 10 – The Morning After Pill

Quickly sitting up, Michael awoke to see he was still in bed. *Dude you're fuckin crazy.* Realizing his immediately previous experience was just a dream, he laid back as a fountain of guilt flooded into his stomach and up into his heart.

What the fuck…I can't fuckin stand this…

So go jump off a bridge then…

No, fuck that…

So shut the fuck up then…

Man, fuck this, I'm goin to the gym.

You think the gym is gonna help. You can't escape this. This is who you are. Just accept it. You were born this way, and you'll be this way till you die.

Nah dude, I can change…

You might be able to change some things, but deep down you'll always be the psycho we both know you are.

You know what, maybe you're right, maybe I am fuckin insane, but you're just as insane as me.

Yeah I know, cuz I Am you…I'm that part of you that gives you the courage to fight.

Yeah, but what am I fighting for? Am I just gonna keep fantasizing about the same shit? If so, what's the point?

The point is that you can have anything you want, all you gotta do is take it.

But that's not right.

Bullshit. Right and wrong don't mean anything. You know that.

I know, but it just doesn't feel right.

It doesn't feel right because you make it not feel right. All you gotta do is forget that part of you that has it not feel right and I can have my way.

Yeah, you're right, I can have my way…nah, nah, fuck that.

Okay, fuck that then, you're a worthless piece of shit, do you like that better. Another surge of guilt flooded Michael's stomach as he sat up to shake the insanity from his head.

I can't keep doin this to myself. Standing up he walked into the bathroom, turned on the shower, stripped down and stepped into the tub. *Just take this shower and let it all go.*

Focusing only on the movements, trying not to think about anything, Michael consciously moved from one action to another. First wetting his hair, then grabbing the soap, then squeezing some into his hand. *Hey that kind a looks like what I did all over Elyssa's face...man shut the fuck up, just take a shower.*

Taking the soap he rubbed his hands together *I bet that'd feel good on my cock* to get the soap evenly distributed. He moved his hands to his head *yeah that would feel good wouldn't it* and he began massaging the soap onto his scalp.

Feeling his fingers rub over his scalp, an image of him masturbating surfaced in his mind. Instantly he began to feel a rise down below. *Nah dude, just take the shower.*

Nah wait, maybe I do need to release myself...yeah release yourself.

Nah, just take the shower. Finished scrubbing his scalp he put his hands under the water to rinse them off, followed by his head. Turning around, he leaned over backwards to let the water run down the back of his head.

Still feeling a warm sensation in his groin *just jerk it dude, what's it gonna hurt* he reached for the bar of soap to begin washing the body. Starting with the face he lathered the bar between his hands *just think how good that would feel if that was your cock* to build lather to scrub his face.

Seeing an image of pleasuring himself in his mind as he scrubbed his face he began to become more erect. *No, I ain't gonna do it.*

He moved his head under the flow of water to rinse his face. Pulling his head out of the water he reached again for the bar of soap. Grabbing it he moved his hand up to his neck and began soaping the body. Moving from his neck to the shoulders, then down each arm, up to the armpit, down the rib cage, across his stomach and over to the other rib cage he scrubbed.

Taking the bar he reached behind him to get some soap on the back. Lathering as much as he could with the bar in his hands, he was only concerned with getting soap on his body. Setting the soap down he again reached behind to get the spots he couldn't reach with the bar.

Finished with that phase of the process he moved in under the water to rinse. Standing under the water he looked down and noticed his penis swollen in size *go ahead, grab a hold* but not yet erect. Almost unconsciously, he reached and squeezed his penis to add life to what was already happening.

Nah, I told myself I wasn't gonna and I'm not gonna...

Well, I'm already there, I might as well...what's it gonna hurt, it's not like you're rapin anybody. Like you do in your dreams. He felt guilt rise, and then his heart hardened.

Yeah, why not.

Reaching for the conditioner he squeezed a little into his hand *remember just a little, you like it kinda rough* as he became ever-increasingly erect in anticipation for what was to come. "There, that's better," he said to himself as he began to slowly massage the conditioner up and down the erection. "Just give into it," he unknowingly whispered to himself. *Just feel how good it feels. That's all that matters.*

Dude, what are you doing to yourself he thought as he snapped into the realization that he was doing exactly what he didn't want to do. *Just keep goin, it feels too good to stop.*

But what about…it doesn't matter, just feel how good it feels, go faster. Immediately he began to go faster, *see how good it feels, go faster.* Increasing speed he felt an urge begin to build at the base of his spine and start to move towards the release point, *yeah, go faster…nah, hold it in…nah, go faster, just let it explode.*

Seconds later, a surge of pleasure erupted as fluid oozed from the tip. *Yeah, see how good this feels* his body quivered in excitation. *Why wouldn't you want to do this.*

Breathing slowly, Michael felt energy flush out of his body as he continued to squeeze every last drop of pleasure out and into the tub.

See, now don't you feel relieved from the dreams we just had, its not bad, I just needed to release some pressure…I still don't want to dream that shit anymore…I don't want those things, I care about people now…they're just dreams, it's not like they're real…do what you want when you're awake, and do what I want when I'm asleep. It's all good, nobody is gonna know unless I tell them.

No, what matters is love, what matters is peace, what matters is that I don't have these insane cravings anymore…I mean fuck, I wrote a book that talks about moving with lust as bein a limitation to true love…then I have these dreams, and now I'm here pleasuring myself…I'm a hypocrite…that's okay to be a hypocrite, everybody is, I'm no different, so what if you're just like the rest of the world.

No man, fuck that. I'm better than that…no I'm not…Yes I am…nah, I just like to think I am…fuck this.

Michael reached down shut off the shower, threw open the curtain, grabbed the towel and quickly dried himself off. He stepped into his shorts lying on the floor, pulled them up to his waist, tied them and made his way back into the bedroom.

Seeing a vision of a basketball in his mind *yeah, I'm goin to the gym* he grabbed his ball, walked to the front door, and grabbed the car keys.

"Hey Mike, where ya goin," his mom asked.

Looking away from her eyes to hide his shame, he turned and said, "goin to shoot hoops, you mind if I take the car?"

"No. Hey, I'm gonna make some cabbage soup tonight, d'ya want some?"

"Yeah, that sounds good. I see ya later alright."

"Bye."

"Bye son," his dad said as he started to wake up from his afternoon nap.

Making his way down the stairs he felt a sucking feeling begin to pull on his chest and into his stomach.

What the fuck am I, he thought as depression began to fill his entire body. *I just need a gun, and I can take care of all this.*

NO, a voice thundered from the back of his mind as he felt a flow of electricity run up his spine. *Fuck it. Go shoot hoops.*

Pulling up to the gym he once spent countless hours training for football in *I wonder what it would've been like if I played basketball in college, I'm better than any of these motherfuckers here…ah well, on with life.*

Making his way into the old gym he saw a few people doing plyometrics. *Ooh hey, volleyball players, I wonder…nope, fuck that, just shoot, forget them.*

Moving to the far side of the court he walked to a few feet directly in front of the hoop and began his routine of fundamentals. Ten one armed shots directly in front, ten to each side, then back up a few feet and repeat.

Finishing that routine, he entered into the next phase consisting of a hundred free throws. Shot after shot he brought his mind into one focus, the front of the rim as he visualized the ball going through the hoop, feeling it happen.

1...2...3 he counted in his mind as he dribbled his routine dribbles. Spinning the ball out in front of him *perfect...perfect...perfect* he thought as he snatched the ball on its return bounce.

Breathe...relax...feel it...let it flow, he said as he began descending into the rhythm of his shot. Effortlessly the ball flew from his hand as he released. Still focusing on the front of the rim he saw the ball sail into the air through his peripheral vision.

"sstp," the net said as the ball fell through perfectly, only grazing the net.

See, everything is alright a voice said in his mind. *Just keep shooting.*

He continued to shoot free throws until he felt a thirst in the back of his throat. Making his way to the water fountain he noticed a few wrestlers in the weight room intensely engaged in their workouts. *That's what I'm talking about, focus.* Getting a quick drink he made his way back into the gym.

Walking up to the ball, he lightly set his foot on top and quickly stepped down as the ball spun onto the top of his toes. He flicked his foot upwards as the ball shot up into the air. He reached out and pushed it forward with his hand.

In the same moment, he accelerated to a sprint as he dribbled towards the middle of the lane from baseline right. Reaching the lower block he snatched the ball out of the air with his right hand while leaping into the air. Grabbing the ball with both hands, he raised it above his head then down behind, an instant later he smashed it through the rim as he purposely pulled as hard as he could on the rim to shake the backboard.

Grabbing the ball from the net as it exited on his way down, he sprinted to the other corner. Tapping where the three point line meets the baseline with his toe, he turned and sprinted towards the lane. Again he leaped and smashed it through as before.

Running from side to side, dunking it every time on his way through the lane, he began to get his heart pumping, to warm up for the workout to come.

A few dunks later, the ball hit the back of the rim and sailed into the air towards the top of the key. Landing, he turned and ran towards it. Grabbing the ball as he jump stopped, setting his pivot foot, he brought the ball through from right to left in a sweep as he visualized defenders arms reaching in to take the ball.

Bringing his arms back towards the right, he faked and quickly moved left as he threw the ball out in front. Snatching the ball a step later and leaping after another step, he raised the ball up and back as he tomahawked it down through the rim.

Landing, he stood there. His breath rapid. Sweat forming on his brow. He looked at the ball as it bounced in front of him. And in that moment, nothing else mattered.

Snatching the ball mid bounce, he casually walked to the three point line at the right side baseline. Spinning the ball out if front of him shuffled his feet back behind the three-point line as he reached out and grabbed the ball as it bounced back into the air. Seconds later it was sailing towards the rim in a high arc, down through the rim it flew. *Ah, nothin but net.*

For the next several hours, Michael lost himself in his first true meditation, basketball. Nothing else mattered as he lost himself in the activity. Over the years he grew accustom to the focus required to be at the level of skill he expected of himself.

He did it for no other reason than to be good at something. What he found in that desire to be good at something was the meditative state his mind entered into as he trained. He allowed nothing else to enter. His only focus was on enhancing his skill.

For countless hours, he would do nothing but visualize and focus on the ball going through the hoop. Letting no other thought enter. His mind zoned into a thoughtless state. In some moments, he didn't even have to visualize anything, just feel the feeling associated with perfection and it guided him completely.

It was peaceful to him, to drive his body into complete exhaustion as his mind was focused only on the ball, the court, and the hoop. He didn't have to think about himself, others or anything else. No stress, no depression, no insanity.

He looked up at the rim as he stood at the free throw line. *End on a make,* he said to himself. Going through his routine, he sank down and rose back up into full extension as the ball released from his hand. Seconds later it fell straight through the rim unharmed.

Sitting down at the free throw line, his legs throbbed with exhaustion. *Hey, where'r those volleyball players, I wonder if they saw how good I am...no dude, shut the fuck up...you ain't gettin into my head...fuck that and fuck you.*

He sat there for a second, then laid back onto the court. Looking up into the rafters, he closed his eyes as his mind wandered away from the gym into a peaceful nothingness...

.

.

.

arise dear one,
from the suffocation of limitation...
Be Free dear one,
and step into unification,
IT already is
and so are You...
Reveal Truth dear one,
it is within you now...

Journey Within
and Know Your Freedom...

Chapter 11 – A Waking Dream

As he sat down at the computer, *arise from insignificance child...your freedom is upon you now* a feeling began to radiate in his heart. *I feel like writin a blog.* Moving the mouse, he watched the cursor glide across the screen to an icon of a Firefox. Double clicking the icon, the web browser initiated its routine until it stopped loading and he sat facing the Google home page.

Control L he said to himself, *www.myspace.com* he thought as he typed it into the URL box. Waiting for the login screen to appear he began to contemplate what to write about. *Ah there we go* as the cursor blinked in the box designated for the email.

mjaye3@gmail.com, he typed into the box. *19830220mj* he said to himself in his mind as he typed in the password. *I wonder if anybody left any comments...does it matter...yeah, kinda, I wanna see what people are saying...what if they say its shit,* instantly a feeling of fear surfaced in his gut. *Well, I don't know, everybody is entitled to their opinion, I'm just writing, and if people feel it helps them, then I've done my job, and so far, the response has been good, so I guess its whatever...yeah, that's what you tell yourself...whatever dude.*

*ooh, hey, new blog comments...*clicking on the link, the 'manage blog' page appeared a few seconds later, *nah, just start writin, forget all that for now.*

Alright what do I write about...2012...2012? why?

just start writing and you'll see...a'ight then, dawg...

What is the significance of 2012? he typed into the keyboard. *I dunno, what is the significance...I know, go research it...ctrl T,* instantly a new tab appeared in the web browser. www.google.com, he typed into the URL box.

okay, what do I search for. Instantly a thought jumped into his mind, *science 2012…* he typed it into the google search box. A moment later the search results began to appear. *What's this, UCAR…the sun-spot cycle will be 30-50% stronger, 2012…yeah, that sounds like a good read.*

He moved the cursor over the link, **http://www.ucar.edu/news/releases/2006/sunspot.shtml**, and the cursor turned into a pointing finger. He clicked the button on the mouse and an instant later, research began.

Going to school at a Catholic school that took pride in academics, he was no stranger to science. He often found himself remembering his high school science teacher who was one of the bigger influences in his quest for knowledge.

Remembering the yearly science fairs, where he and all his classmates in all grades would have to compose a science project, he often silently thanked her for setting the standard high in recognizing and implementing science. More than that, it was the scientific method that allowed him to come into actually being methodical about how he approached things.

Test and observe was the approach that he learned from his mentor, and it served him well. Science became the key that ultimately unlocked the door of his mind beyond the societal normalcy that he thought existed.

And as he sat there researching sun-spot activity, his mind drifted back to English class during his junior year in high school when he had to decide on a topic for his term paper.

"And when you pick a topic for what you wanna write about," Mrs. Farris said, "maybe think about writing about something that excites you. Also, remember I've been doin this for a lot of years now, and I've read a lot of term papers on a lot of the same topics. So if you think you can slip one by me, you might think about picking a topic that I've never read about."

He didn't want to disappoint. Sitting in class that day, an image ran though his mind of all his older brothers going through this same process from the same teacher. So as he began to contemplate about what to write, he asked himself, "what is the one thing that nobody has ever written a term paper about."

From that question, his mind drifted to outer space. So he began to look through books until he narrowed it down to one topic, "black holes".

And while sitting there remembering this while he was researching about 2012, he realized that the groundwork for this journey he was on had been laid since before he realized. *I guess I always just kinda gravitated towards the mysterious*, he thought as he clicked back over to the myspace blog editor.

So he began to type, Recently, scientists and the National Center for Atmospheric Research forecast a prediction for the year 2012...*Yeah, that sounds about right* in which the sun will reach an apex of energetic activity. The energetic activity is said to be 30-50 percent...*do I put the percent sign or do I spell it out...ah, yeah, I want this to appear as more formal, spell it out* more intense than the apex of the last cycle.

As he continued to write, that feeling in his heart that initiated the vision to write in the first place began to grow, so he continued.

So what is the significance about the year 2012? Well, approximately 4000 years ago, a group of people known as the Mayans were existing. They then proceeded to design a calendar that mysteriously stops in 2012...*well it wasn't just the mayans either, hell, almost all religions talk about an end times...*

Not only the Mayans, but the Aztecs, the Hopis, and almost all religions on the face of the earth refer to this time as the "end-times."

Coincidence? *is it a coincidence,* he thought to himself. *What if it is...just keep writing dude, it will all become more clear.*

Well, consider this, in an article by David Wilcock, "A Scientific Blueprint for Ascension," he notes that volcanic activity has increased by 500 percent within the last 30 years, and that earthquake activity has increased 400 percent in that same time frame. He also notes that between 1963 and 1993, natural disasters increased by 410 percent.

yeah, that is kind of a bit much to all be coincidence...

well, you know, it only holds true if all those numbers are accurate...

yeah, and the only way I can actually deny those numbers is if I do all those tests myself, and if I do that, what good is science...that's what it's for, is to present data that is as objective as it can be. I have to trust that he did the research and that the ones who did the experiments did the research within an acceptable margin of error...otherwise I'm just reinventing the wheel if I go back and re-work all the data. This is faith as much as any religion.

yeah, well David Wilcock isn't really a real scientist...

does that actually matter...

yeah...

why…
cuz he didn't get his degree like all those other guys…
yeah, and?…
well, he…
just face it, he knows his shit..did bill gates graduate, exactly, so what does a degree really mean? Dick shit.

As Michael finished his internal dialogue he realized he hadn't written anything in the mean time. *Goodness gracious, just be slient and write…who cares about all that other shit that doesn't mean anything, just say what you need to say, get it out, and you will see.*

He continued writing, According to Ken Carey in his 'Starseed Transmissions: Starseed the Third Millennium'

Five centuries before the dawn of the present era, in the jungles of the Yucatan, we brought to the Awakened Ones of that age a timetable, which they carefully recorded in stone. The Mayan Calendar is recovered now from moss, fern, lizard and leaf. In it are chiseled the dates of the Great Purification, dates that correspond to your years, 1987 to 2011. The winter solstice of the last year of this intensified twenty-five year cycle will see the purification complete, the era of human history brought forever to a close.

What? The era of human history brought to a close, what the is that suppose to mean Michael thought. A moment a later a voice responded, *it doesn't matter, that is the future, free yourself now and you need not worry about it…alright then, write.*

If the increases in the activity of the earth in the recent years are not "purification," what is it?

Coincidence? *how many times am I gonna write coincidence? am I playin that card to much…does it matter…no, I guess not…so keep writing.*

David Wilcock also goes on to note that research being done by The Russian National Academy of Sciences in Siberia has shown that our solar system is moving into a position of higher energetic influence.

Wilcock says that there has been a 1000 percent increase in the energy at the "leading edge" of our solar system. *what does that mean…does it matter…no, I guess not…so keep writing.*

According to The Keys of Enoch (1973), by J.J. Hurtak, "While I was in the act of prayer, calling upon the name of the Father, asking to know the meaning of life" he was presented the following revelation.

> There is presently occurring a space-time overlap with the 'Higher Evolution' as the Earth's solar system enters an electromagnetic null zone, a vacuum area in space which will

change the magnetic forces of creation.

The change of the electromagnetic density in the Earth's atmosphere will activate some species to become more violent and other species to become more Christ-like as man is pulled either into an upward spiral of Light or negated by the breakdown of the old electromagnetic frequency. This will bring about a complete reorganization of Earth's life system...

Before the new story of creation happens, the Earth will go through gross geo-magnetic and catastrophic changes as the magnetic regions of the North and South Pole release 'their torque,' spinning the shell (surface crust) of the Earth into the new program of existence.

And it will occur after the wars between the Sons of Light versus the Sons of Darkness that a 'New Age' will occur for all of mankind surviving the great changes.

There is a forming of the new worlds at this time for there is

to be soon existent new planets…
The Nine shall place upon the new
realms those 'physical souls' who
have perfected themselves upon the
Earth plane. Those souls who have
evolved to the highest point of
advancement on Earth shall be of
the New Creation.

The younger souls of the
faithful who survive the old
program will become the physical
seed of the Christ people upon the
planet. The faithful who are
already initiated into the many
gifts will be taken to other
planets. This will come to pass
only after the unrighteous are
removed from the face of the
earth. At that time the earth will
be in a new electromagnetic orbit
and there will be new heavens and
new earth.

Really, Michael thought, *all that shit's gonna happen…no, it's already happening, and the more you release the binds of your mind you can see the truth of what is important in your soul. These changes mean nothing in comparison to what is within you…just keep writing…fine then, I'll keep writing.*

If you consider what David Wilcock has
noted about the earth moving farther away
from the sun, which is also noted in ancient

calendars by the addition of five and a quarter days.

That is, as the earth moves away it "break(s) into higher levels of vibration represented by a bigger sphere." Also noting what geologists call "punctuated equilibrium," which is "at about 50-million-year intervals all life that had been on the Earth spontaneously dies. And then, all of a sudden, this higher order creature shows up."

Huh, that's kinda cool...just keep writing. Wilcock also notes the "study published by Dr. Bruce Runnegar and other UCLA astrobiologists who supports the theory. The researchers looked at planetary orbits and ran them back through time with computer simulations, they discovered that 65 million years ago, at the time of the most recent mass extinction (of the dinosaurs), there was what they referred to as a chaotic change in the resonant frequencies of the Solar System. This chaotic change suddenly jostled all the orbits of the inner planets."

Is it all a coincidence? *there you go with coincidence again* If not, what does all this mean?

Does it mean Rapture and Ascension? Maybe.

Does it mean Evolution and Extinction? Yes.

Does it mean Change? Most definitely!

The change will be evolution into higher levels of consciousness, and extinction of the old ways.

A change from Competition to Co-operation.

A change from dishonesty to integrity.

A change from selfishness to compassion.

A change from fear to love. We will cease to exist in The World of Fear and come to know the unlimitedness of the World of Love.

No longer will fear be the way of life, but rather the love and loveliness of everything.

As Norma Milanovich put it in her book, 'We the Arcturians' (1980s):

> Humankind is just beginning to feel a shift of consciousness resulting in a happier condition… Individuals of higher states of consciousness are beginning to separate themselves from those individuals of lower, more angry states. The vibrational frequencies of the two sets of individuals are beginning to clash…this clash will become more obvious.

Planet Earth is beginning to prepare for the cleansing of negative energy that surrounds her. You have already seen the signs with the violent weather changes, volcanoes that have erupted and will continue to erupt, earthquakes, and the changing ozone layer...The energy of humankind has polluted beloved Terra long enough. The cleansing will be complete.

You see, each planet and star system goes through similar periods of trials and errors as the Earth is doing right now. We are here to help one of the most difficult birthing processes that has ever been the challenge to any of the Beings of the universe.

The people of Earth are on a path that is irreversible. On this journey, they must realize that Light and Love are the only two qualities that can be adhered to for advancement into the New Age.

But souls must choose which one they will master. There are only two choices: there is Love and Light, or there is fear. Choose, our dearest brothers and sisters

of the universe. And make this
choice before the portal of time
into this new dimensional
frequency closes and makes the
choice for you.

That's pretty fatalistic, one or the other, is that fair, Michael thought.
*It is what it is, it is neither here nor there, you have known fear for far too long
and you are well aware of its effects. Choose love and open into something far more
profound than you have ever imagined possible.* With that thought, a flood of
energy broke loose in his heart and he was unable to move. Closing
his eyes, he focused more deeply on that feeling. As he did, it shot up
his spine and out the top of his head and he was overcome with an
indescribable bliss. *Just keep writing,* a voice whispered in his mind.

Opening his eyes, Therefore, he typed, in these
times of "chaos" we must make a stand with
fear, or a stand with love.

It is a revolutionary moment that takes
a revolutionary stance. We can embrace the
fear, violence, subjugation and decay of
death.

Or, we can embrace the love, happiness,
bliss, abundance and eternity of life.

The choice is yours, do with it what
you will.

I ask that if you choose love, you
bring this message to others, and give them
awareness of the choice at hand. I ask for
your help in embracing this New Age. If you
agree to the power of love, I ask that you
repost this, email this, send it out to
those who may not be aware of the times in

126

which we find ourselves. We can make a
difference, but it can only be together.

OneLuv
Your Brother

P.S. Want to read more about the power of
love, then visit and read the blog at
http://www.myspace.com/LeaveYourEgoAtTheDoor

Feeling complete, Michael began taking the necessary actions to see the entry posted onto the blog. *I wonder what people will say,* he thought as he began re-reading the finished product. *It doesn't matter, all I can do is present them with what I see and it is their choice to discern and embrace what is there for them. They have free-will just as I.*

Chapter 12 – Salvation

"Are you ready?" Michael heard a voice in the crowd say.

hecks yeah I'm ready he thought as he turned to look for who said it, *this is what I'm here for.*

Michael noticed a short white man standing just out of the crowd, straight faced, staring directly at his eyes. Michael began to make his way through the middle of the crowd, and as he neared the short man, he reached out a hand to Michael.

He grabbed the hand of the man who proceeded to pull Michael to stand with him outside of the crowd.

Looking down onto the top of the man's freshly shaved head, he quickly moved his eyes to interact with the deep blue eyes of the man.

An intense gaze pierced its way from the man's eyes straight into Michael's soul as the man said, "I am honored for you to be here."

A warm feeling began to arise in Michael's chest. *who is this guy*, Michael thought.

"May I ask you a question," the man said.

"yeah," Michael replied.

"Are you ready" he asked.

Taking a moment to consider the question, Michael then said, "Yeah I'm ready, I'm always ready."

"How do you know you're ready," the man quickly replied.

"I don't know, I just kinda feel it. Like a feeling in the stomach I guess, the hands kinda buzz, a warm movement up the spine."

"So, are you ready" the man again asked.

"Yeah, I just told you, I'm ready."

"Okay," he said, "if you're ready, what are you standing for?"

Michael thought for a moment *love...duh,* "I'm standing for Love."

The man then asked, "who is I?"

Michael looked at the man with a perplexed stare. The man again spoke, "To what do you refer to when you say 'I'?"

thats a great question Michael thought. *who Is I? I refer to two different things as 'I', one is me the body and one is me the spirit...so which one is I?... damn... this joker got me thinking deep n shit.* "I would have to say that I is who I really am, but who that is, I don't know."

The man smiled, "Isn't it funny how we often throw the word 'I' around as if it is yesterday's trash. What if we held it as a sacred vocalization of who we really are?"

A sacred vocalization...huh, what if. "You know," Michael said, "yeah, a sacred vocalization. I like that." *who is this guy?*

"Okay, Brother," the man said to Michael, "Are you ready to take a stand? And I'm talking, A STAND," the man's voice roared.

Tingles began sprinkling up and down Michael's spine as he squirmed to let the sensations flow more freely. "Yeah dude, yeah."

The man positioned his feet shoulder width apart, "Feet shoulder width apart," he said. Taking a long deep breath in, "take a deep breath, and, just get present."

Following the instruction, Michael positioned the body accordingly then inhaled and slowly exhaled. He began to feel sensations all over his body as his eyes softly gazed just over the top of the crowd that had thinned out to a few passing by.

"Imagine your standing in front of a mountain," the man said. "Look up the mountain," he said while pointing to an imaginary mountain top right in front of him.

Michael glanced over at the man standing next to him pointing to the top of the imaginary mountain in front of him.

"Look," the man said, pointing up in the air. "Before you is everything that you will face on the path you are walking, are you ready to journey to the mountain top?"

"Yes!" Michael replied.

"Take another deep breath. Now, what are you feeling as you face your mountain?"

"Uh, a fear, yeah definitely fear... apathy, doubt." Pausing for a moment, "yeah, those are pretty apparent to me right now."

"Good," he said. "Now are you ready to move through them to the other side?"

"Yes!"

"Now, when you are feeling fear, what is the thought or story you are telling yourself?" he asked Michael.

"Uh, well, that I'm not ready enough, that there's more I gotta learn, that I'm not as powerful as I think I am, that people are gonna laugh at me..."

"Okay, okay, what about apathy, what are the thoughts?" he asked.

"That I don't really care, that I can't really make a difference anyway, that people don't change, the world is too effed up, life sucks and then you die, there's no point cuz its hopeless...uh, It's not my job to make a difference..."

"Okay, and what about doubt?"

Michael took a deep, "that I'm not ready, that this is too big for me, I can't do it alone..."

The man paused for a moment, inhaled slowly, then said, "Okay, so let's do this. One more big breath."

Michael slowly inhaled, filling his lungs completely, then slowly began to exhale as a sense of calm began to wash over his body.

The man looked at Michael, "repeat after me, then fill in the blanks."

"Okay."

"In the face of feeling..."

Michael looked at the man gesturing that it was now his turn. "In the face of feeling fear," he said as he looked at the man to see if he was doing it right. The man gently nodded his head gesturing yes. "...doubt, apathy, fear..."

"When I narrate..." the man said on cue.

"When I narrate that I'm not ready enough, that I don't really care, that I'm not as powerful as I think, that the world is too effed up." Michael glanced over to the man for the next cue.

The man paused for a moment, "in this next part, there are no limitations on being." He took a deep breath, brought his right hand to his chest in a swift movement, making a thud as his hand slapped his chest, "I...Stand...For Being..." he roared as the earth shook from the depth of his voice.

Beginning to mimic the man's movements, Michael inhaled slowly, and moved his hand to his chest as demonstrated. "I... Stand... For Being," Michael paused, smiled, then continued, "For Being a pure conduit of Unconditional Love." He paused for a moment as he became aware of an intense warmth in his chest while his legs felt as if buried to the center of the earth, and his shoulders flying above the clouds.

Not knowing what to make of it, Michael glanced towards the man standing next to him who was wearing a wide smile. Continuing to breathe, Michael just let the experience soak in.

"What are you experiencing?" the man asked.

"Uh, Love, Power, Freedom."

The man smiled even wider, "try on Honor."

"Yeah, definitely, yeah..."

"What are you seeing?"

"Oh my god, like infinite possibilities, the earth completely born a new, people all over the world waking up to their true potential, birds singing louder, the sun shining brighter, grass growing taller."

"Are you inspired?"

"Inspired isn't even the word bro, take that times a trillion, then you got it."

"How does it feel to take a stand?"

"Liberating." Michael stood motionless, continuing to soak in the experience through every breath. The man stood next to him, still smiling as a tear began to roll from his eye.

"I am honored that you are here, Brother," the man said as his eyes pierced once again into Michael's soul.

"Likewise Brother," Michael replied. "May I ask what name you use."

"Michael, Michael Skye."

wouldn't ya know it, what'r the odds of that, another Michael Michael thought as he smiled love into the eyes of his newly found soul brother. "I am honored to embrace your Presence, Michael. Thank you for you."

Michael watched as he saw his newly found brother turn towards the crowd and smile. His brother looking back into Michael's eye's, winking, then nodding his head towards the crowd while opening his eyes wide, as if gesturing to Michael it is time to wake up all our brother's and sister's.

Smiling back to his brother, Michael softly laughed in agreement. "I'm gonna go start with my family and friends if that's cool with you."

"Of course bro," Michael Skye responded, "That's where its gotta start. Take it one day at a time, be present with everyone you meet and honor is given room to flow."

"Thank you for opening my eyes brother, and thank you for giving me your love. Thank you for being the example, and thank you for standing for everyone." Michael reached into to hug his brother, leaning down and picking him for a heart to heart hug, he gave his brother a bear hug.

Setting him down, they both looked deeply into the eyes and smiled. Winking while turning, Michael stepped back into the flow of the crowd. As he did, a path in the crowd opened up before him. Easily flowing with the movements of the crowd, Michael continued walking down the sidewalk smiling into the eyes of everyone who looked into his.

As he continued walking, he noticed a lightness in his steps, almost as if he was floating on air as he walked down the side walk *i wonder if this is how Jesus walked on water* he thought to himself. Smiling at the vision of Jesus walking along side him, a deep peace radiated from his heart.

Seeing a park bench a few yards up, Michael made his way to the bench and sat down to sit and be with the energy in his heart.

Thank You Jesus.

Chapter 13 – Dialoguing with The Devil

Hey, let's have some fun...
What kinda fun...
You know, fun. A vision of a naked woman flashed in his vision as pleasure arose in his member of manhood. Darkness swirled around him as he found himself waking up inside a bus he didn't remember entering. "Where am I?"

On the fun train a voice whispered in his mind. Michael rose to get off the bus. As he reached the driver's seat, the door slammed shut. *Nope, it's not gonna be that easy young man. This is my adventure ride, and you're on it till the last stop.*

Suddenly the bus lurched forward, throwing Michael backward down the aisle. He twisted to the right landing in a seat, bashing his head against the side of the bus. His internal light of consciousness dimmed for a moment. As he gained his senses, he was no longer on a bus, but in a hallway of what seemed like a medical facility that had been abandoned for many years.

With no one in sight, he began to search for an exit. Continuing to walk down the corridor, he peered through a dirt stained window girded by iron bars, to see a sign outside that read, "Home for the Psychologically Affected".

What in god's great name does that mean he thought to himself.

"Welcome home, Michael," he heard a voice say.

"Yeah, Not!"

"Haha, what you don't realize, Michael, is this place is where you have been for most of your life, you have just failed to recognize the extent to which you are truly home."

"Where are you so I can shut you up?"

"You're proving my point for me, young man."

This is a dream he thought to himself. An electricity shot up his spine as he came to this clarity. *So this isn't real.*

"It may not be physically real, but that doesn't mean it's real nonetheless. Your mind creates your state of living. You are in the darkest parts of your mind, Michael. What you see here is all your creation. This is You. Proceed wisely, my son."

"I'm not your son you sadistic asshole."

"Ha, I'm more a part of you than you may realize. You'll see soon enough."

"Where are you and we can make this quick?"

Silence permeated the air. He continued walking. The voice returned no answer. *Whatever, if this is a dream I can just wake up…wake up mike, wake up…hahaha, it's not that easy…hey, fuck you, get outta my head…don't you realize by now, I am you.*

His gut began wrenching as his heart dropped 6 inches to the point of feeling on the verge of being sick. *Now you're starting to realize just what situation you have found yourself. Here's a tip, don't deny it. Accept it for who you are, and this journey will be much less painful for you.*

"FUCK OFF CLOWN."

"Yes, that's it. Feel the anger. Let it move you."

As he continued walking down a long corridor of empty rooms to one side and a cloudy sunlight shining through iron bars on the other, he approached a doorway with a sign above that said, "Sexual Deviant Wing."

His heart fluttered as he walked through the door. Images began pouring through his mind, as if being attacked by the imagery soaked up and stored by the building's walls. The emotions of all the patients that have ever lived here oozing from every crack. Suddenly he noticed sexual excitement being to rise in him.

Yes, that's it, let it flow.

Fuck you.

That works too. Come see me big boy and you may have your wish granted.

Alright mike, just breathe, this isn't real. Stop where you are, and breathe. Taking in three long, slow, deep breaths, he found an equilibrium begin to resonate in his solar plexus. The wrenching of his gut began to subside.

There's no need to fight this, Michael, this is who you are.

NO. THIS, IS NOT, who I am.

No, take a left into room 13 if you really want to challenge yourself on this.

He quickly moved forward to room 13. As he pushed the door open he found his young teenage self, sitting at a computer. Circling back to get a view of what his teenage self was looking, he noticed that the young man was unaware of anything but the computer screen. As he reached a spot to see the screen, he noticed his teenage self was absorbed in viewing pornography.

Another surge of pleasure rose through him.

Still doubt me.

"I acknowledge that my past was laden with heavy porn use. But that is not part of my future."

No. Then why do you find yourself stopping to view any image you see anywhere that has any degree of sexual overtones. I mean, you know full well the marketing tactic behind "Sex Sells". And yet, you willingly perpetuate that in yourself.

The wrenching returned to his gut as he recognized the taste of guilt on his tongue. *You need not fear your sexual desire Michael, make it your closest friend and you will be free from this guilt.*

"Fuck you." He quickly moved to the exit, stubbing his toe on the desk as he did. "Shit." *Good lord I cuss too much.*

Why are you running from yourself. There's no need to avoid it any longer, embrace this side of you and you will receive everything you've ever fantasized about.

Another surge of pleasure pulsed throughout his groin as an image flashed in his mind of having his way with a woman of refined beauty. "I'm your sex slave. Do with me what you want," he heard an auditory voice ring throughout the halls. "Come to me, come in me, come on me."

The pleasure magnified in his body.

"No!"

Why fight it, Michael? You can feel in yourself that you desire these things.

He's right. I do have this desire… no, Michael, this is not yours, it was given to you without your consent.

Wait, what, who said that?

"Just feel the desire, Michael, see what you want to do to her in your mind. This is all possible if only you embrace your true nature."

"Shut The Fuck Up, will you!" *goodness, I need to really stop cussing… wait, why am I worrying about curse words at a time like this…* Michael shook his head free of the last thought.

"Hahahaha, if I shut up, you shut up. I am you," the voice echoed. "I'm the part of you that you have tried to deny exists. I'm that which can give you everything you desire if only you surrender to my will."

"Your will, or my will? I thought you we're me. Why would you describe it as your will and not mine? Huh, asshole?"

"I see you want to play that game. Why don't you take a right up ahead, and proceed until you see a sign that says, 'Deepest Desires'. Then we'll really see whose will it really is."

"Is that a challenge? Like, you're trying to pique my curiosity by challenging me? You must know me fairly well, I admit. Challenge accepted. And guess what, I'm going to prove your clown-ass wrong."

Determination pulsing through his body, Michael moved forward down the hall. He soon found himself facing the doorway. A fluttering of butterflies swam through his stomach.

Is that doubt I sense in you Michael?

Taking a deep breathe, he focused his mind on his goal, and dropped his energy to the center of the earth in preparation to bring up a shield of energy.

His mind suddenly flashed back to being announced as starting QB before one of his high school football games, and noticed the electricity he felt then was the same as he felt now. "I'm gonna crush this bitch."

Standing before the door entering into the ward of Deepest Desires, *no sense in being stealthy, he already knows I'm here.* He took a step back, preparing to kick the door.

He focused on the door right next to the handle, and launched forward with his left foot. The door frame snapped, bursting open, as Michael was sucked forward in a release of vacuum pressure. Tumbling into the ward, he rolled to a stop and quickly noticed he was standing on a rocky floor. Looking to his right, he noticed walls as if in a cave. Same to the left. Above his head was a tall cavern reaching hundreds of feet upward. Looking back, he saw no sign of the door he just entered through. Only a long cave stretching into darkness.

"What the fuck!"

"This is your true home. The place you have been searching to find your whole life," the voice vibrated off the walls deep in resonance.

"Uh, no. This is definitely not my home. If it was, I'd have graffiti art all over these walls. You be slippin' home slice."

"Come find me. Go ahead and take a walk down the rabbit holes of this underground dungeon of yours."

He took a step forward and as soon as his first step touched the ground, he began to hear moans. The moans were not of pain, but of pleasure. He began to feel the pleasure in his body. In a moment, his body was enveloped in the pleasures of orgasm, both a masculine and feminine energy.

He felt the energy nearing climax. Instantly, he was erect. A moment later, release.

And the shrieks of pleasure began undulating through the cave. Each surge of the masculine energy was followed by an explosion of the feminine. Grunting, panting, and shrill moaning echoed throughout.

Breathe, Michael, this energy is not yours.

"Can you feel it Michael, just take it all in. Let yourself marinate in these energies. This is your domain."

He stopped, shook his head of the images pouring through his mind, and took a deep breath down into his belly. He felt the grip on his sword. *Wait, what, when did I get this sword… and it's a blue light for a blade.* As he exhaled, he began praying, *Holy Michael, the Archangel, defend us in battle. Be our safeguard against the wickedness and snares of the devil. May God rebuke him, we humbly pray; and do you, O Prince of the heavenly host, by the power of God cast into hell Satan and all the evil spirits who wander through the world seeking the ruin of souls.*

He took another step, nothing happened. He continued moving forward, slowly. He gripped the sword with both hands as he ventured ever deeper into the cavern of Desire.

Be ever vigilant in discerning what is yours, and what is not yours, Michael.

Gratitude swelled in his heart for Archangel Michael. *I don't know if you here, Michael, or if that was you, but thank you for being a guiding light in this battle.*

The silence in the air penetrated into his bones. *This is too silent. Too calm.* An image of bear trap flashed in his mind. *Yeah, probably so.*

He continued forward. The cave walls veered to the right. As he arced around, he sensed it was at about a 90 degree angle from the direction he was previously heading. Several more paces forward, he began to see a fork in the path emerge.

Well crap. He remembered a wise wizard once saying, "When in doubt follow your nose." Standing before the fork, he reached into himself and sensed for the guidance of his heart. An aroma of vanilla bean wafted up from the left, while the stench of sewer came from the right.

Left it is.

The path narrowed as the cavernous space above shrank away into a confined tunnel just tall enough so he could stand without ducking.

Well isn't that interesting how the cave is just big enough for your tall ass. Don't ya think, Michael.

Your tricks are ill attempted Master of Darkness. This is a dream, and it can shift at a moment's notice. This matrix of yours holds me not.

As he continued moving forward, a hole in the left side of the wall appeared out of the darkness. Iron bars caged the entrance to what appeared to be a room. Arms suddenly surged out the bottom, "Take me, I go willingly." The figure of a nude woman rose to standing. "I will fulfill your every desire," she said as she reached to massage her wetness. Reaching up she said, "Taste me, you will not be disappointed."

Desire exploded in his groin as the fragrance of femininity entered his space. *Breathe.* Turning his head to the side, he closed his eyes, and took a deep breath, allowing the desire to be, while removing the narrative that he must taste this woman.

"No, that is not for me. I am vowed to a woman who honors and respects herself. This is clearly something you must learn." Empathy rose in his heart as he peered into the woman's eyes. Instantly, her smile faded as tears emerged. "You are free, child. Give yourself to no one until you find that place in yourself where you live in honor and respect for the sacredness of your femininity." As he spoke, the erection he had waned, and the perspective of this woman shifted from a sex slave, to a human female ensnared by the trappings of man.

Michael looked to the lock on the iron bars, then to his sword of blue light. *Hmmm.* "Stand back." He rose the sword in the air and swung at the lock. It melted as if it was air. The bars disintegrated as the woman turned to a field of light waving in the air. A moment later, she was gone.

Release them from your hold as you go.

"What, release who from my hold?" *All that you see here has been repressed in your psyche, and acts as attachments to real people. Go with wisdom.*

"Michael, Michael, Michael," a voice droned. "Tsk, tsk. You are not giving satisfaction to your desires. Why do you deny yourself this pleasure?"

"Because I choose integrity."

"We'll see. We shall see," the voice jeered. "Keep following that nose of yours and come find me big boy." He ventured on as cages began to appear on his right and left, each with another woman. After several cages, he paused, *release them from this.*

He stood looking back at the cages, and memories of psychically desiring these women throughout his life surfaced in his mind. *Disintegrate the attachment in your heart, and destroy the locks on these cages.* He took a deep breath, imagined a fire in his heart, as he exhaled, beams of light shot from his palms towards the locks. Moments later the locks lay on the floor and the door to the cages swung open. "You are free from these bonds. Please forgive me."

Continuing forward, as he came to a cage, he would breathe light through his hands, say a silent prayer as visions of his what his past exploits flashed through his mind. The cages would open, and a shimmer of light would emerge and fly upward through the ceiling of the cave.

"Michael, you disappoint me. You could have such a great time, if only you would give into that which you hold in your heart."

"You fail to recognize that I hold these things no longer in my heart. If you would open your eyes, you would see that I have released my hold on them," He said progressing forward. "Why don't we make this quick? Show yourself."

"As you wish."

A moment later Michael was standing before a golden throne with a seat of red velvet.

"Really, that's a bit cliché for a throne isn't it? You couldn't have gone with something a little more, I don't know, not 500 years ago?"

"What do you mean, Michael," he heard a voice behind him. Spinning around, sword drawn and up, he stood facing himself, "That seat is yours. You picked it out. I've only been keeping it warm for you."

The pain in his gut spread to his hips, and down to his knees. The stench of sewer filled the air as he waivered where he stood. His vision narrowed and he felt faint. "I sense that you are now understanding the gravity of this situation, Michael. Shall I give you a moment to take it all in?"

Grinding his teeth, he closed his eyes to focus on the feel of the sword's hilt in his hand. Breathing in, he opened his eyes to see them mirrored back by the individual standing before him. "You, are not me, this is a trick."

"Tell me, then, why do you feel what you do you in your stomach if this is a trick? Your worst fear has been realized, you are your own worst enemy."

"No, you are not me. No matter what you try to say, this is no my domain."

"You're denying the inevitable. That caged beast you've been fighting your whole life, that's part of you. I am only a representation of it. Those emotions, desires, thoughts, they're all yours. You produced them. You own them."

"Nooo," Michael yelled as he raised his sword arcing to cut the head off his counter-part. He missed as his evil twin ducked the blade of blue light, as if he knew it was coming.

Quickly snapping the blade back toward his twin's chest, a blade of gold sprang up to stop his stroke. "It will not be that easy, Michael."

The next minute saw a flurry of strokes as Michael went on the attack, backing his evil twin around the throne room. Not once did his twin make for a counter move. Only movements of defense.

"Fight me!" Michael screamed.

"I don't need to. There's no point in it for me. We can end this now. All you need do is accept that I am you and this is over."

He yelled, "I will never accept that," as he snapped into attacking his twin again. Out of the corner of his eye, he saw an iron door locked by a bolt from floor to ceiling. His stomach churned.

Looking back to his twin, he noticed him glance over his shoulder to the door. Looking back at Michael, his twin went on the attack for the first time.

"Looks like you're hiding something from me." Michael parried the stroke. He followed the momentum of the blade as it sliced downward. Turning his wrist, he quickly snapped back and hammered at the guard of his twin's sword. The sword fell to the ground. Michael raised the blue light just under his twin's chin. "Tell me, what's behind that door?"

He took a breath and exhaled as light shot from his palm. Nothing happened. "That, Michael, is your worst nightmare. Something for which you have no recollection. And something for which you are not ready to see."

"Move." Michael jabbed the point of his sword into his twin's sternum. He reached down and grabbed the sword of gold and threw it to the other side of the room. "I'll be the judge of my readiness." He jabbed again, as his twin stumbled backwards towards the locked door.

Reaching the door, "Open it." His twin reached for a key on his waist. "No. Move aside." Michael raised his sword and smashed the lock holding the bolt in place. "Open it."

His twin turned the wheel in the middle of the door. The bolts unlatched from the ceiling and the floor. As soon as they were free, the door gently opened a few inches. "Stand aside."

Michael reached for the door, and swung the door open the rest of the way. The sword fell from his hand as he saw his eight year old self curled up, naked, crying in the corner; oblivious to anything.

He sat up with a startle as he looked around to see he was in his bedroom. Reflecting on the previous moment, he realized he just had a dream. The images from it already began to fade as he tried to play it back from the beginning. His body swam with sensations. Feelings of power, of shame, guilt, lust. Feelings of honor, integrity, love, fear.

He took a deep breath. As he exhaled, he was left with an image of his child-self curled in the corner of a room crying. For some reason the room felt familiar. He felt as if he had known that place but couldn't remember exactly where, or when. The convulsions in his stomach told him he needed to breathe and stretch.

<u>Chapter 14 – Who Am I?</u>

Reaching for the shade, he took a deep breath. Opening the shade, he stood and began moving his body as if a current of liquid was flowing through him. The sun was just beginning to dawn as the night was quickly becoming a thing of the past.

Divine Creator of All that is, he began to pray as he sat at the head of the bed. He held those words as he momentarily envisioned the vastness of existence, vibrating in perfect symmetry. *I've come to understand that there are things in me that I'm confused about. Namely my sexuality.* Tears formed in his eyes as an intense heat burned in his solar plexus that began to well upwards through his lungs. *I have desires and urges that I struggle with daily,* he took a deep breath. *I don't know the full scope of why these things are in me the way they are, but I'm resolved to lead a holy life. I've committed my life to live the message of Jesus Christ, but I'm not quite sure how to do that, or what the full implications of that life entails.*

He stopped verbalizing his thoughts as he reflected on the visions that arose with the last statement. Images of his past began running through his mind. All the situations he ever felt confused about himself, and a brief moment in church, at the retreat he went to his senior year, where his heart felt what he came to know as love. *I am resolved to lead a holy life…* "I know that I don't know everything," he began verbalizing aloud. "I know that I don't know where my future is headed. And I know that I don't know the full extent of Your Will for me on this planet. What I do know is I trust you. *I also know that Love is the Truth of Reality. I feel this in my heart as the pillar of my existence. And I know that living love is the purpose of my life and my actions. You know I'm willing to give my life at moment's notice if the purpose is true and just. And you also know me better than I do.*

Feeling an expansion in his chest, he took a deep breath. "I trust you to show me the way. And I trust you to love me unconditionally. This is who you are for me. You are the foundation of my existence. The air to my breath." Michael paused as a tear rolled from his eye, down his cheek, and stopped at the edge of his chin. He lightly flexed his jaw muscles as he reflected on his life of struggle. Growing up as the youngest of six boys, in a family that earned everything they had. A memory of being 11, living on a pig farm where he and his family took care of pigs in exchange for rent. A moment later, a memory of his cousin committing suicide flashed as he realized he was near the same age for both experiences.

"Divine Creator, I know I've faced adversity in this life, and I know I haven't faced the worst of it. There are many others in this world who have seen worse. I'm grateful that I've come to this place I'm at where I feel my depression lessening, and my joy increasing." A memory of getting a bill from a bill collector flashed through his mind, as the emotional resonance of depression that still laced the memory arose in his stomach. "I cherish the beauty of this vessel you have created for me that is my human body. It is an amazing thing. My life here on this planet, and in this body, is a miracle of Your Creation. Thank you for this experience. It is my purpose to stand illuminated in Your Truth and move as a conduit of Your Being," he began to more formally pray a prayer he wrote.

"Your life flows through me and my consciousness is washed clean by your grace. I accept full responsibility for the actions of my past. Help me to submit to the wisdom that has been revealed to me in them.

"I forgive all others for their actions toward me, and request forgiveness from all others for my actions toward them. I hold full resolution in Grace as the extension of my desire for others. I ask that you hold my mind and heart firm in the space of peace with others. Remind me constantly of Your Grace, forever, from this moment in eternity, Amen."

As Michael continued to resonate in the energy connecting to his higher authority, he focused his mind and heart into the center of his being, calling out to all of creation with his happiness for being alive. *I wonder what other planets look like...* A moment later, *I wonder how many humans exist in the universe.* His heart glowed with pleasure.

A smile curved the corner of his lips. *I think I'd like to be an artist today, a writer to be exact. I shall write a story.* He paused momentarily. *What shall I write about,* he thought.

"Divine Mother, I know that I am a warrior who dreams of peace. I'm not Buddha, I'm not Jesus, and I'm not Gandhi. I will not sit there and let others beat me. I am a warrior born into this world.

"I was born, and soon thereafter, I was given two swords. One for each hand. These swords I carry have become extensions of my own body. I know how to fight. I'm really good at fighting. I know this about myself. I also know that I don't want to fight unless it's justified and necessary. I want peace. I want relationships of harmony, of synergy. But I'm afraid that I'm not sure how to tend that garden. I feel reluctance to lay down my swords, and I'm not sure which tools to pick up instead.

"My solution to fighting has been to be a more ferocious voice to stop the fighting. But if a fight is justified, I'll be the one leading the way. I've come to understand the battle which I cannot lose is the battle that ensues within me. And in many ways, I feel helpless. My whole life has been about force. Watching others get what they want through varying degrees of coercion, as well as seeing myself coerce others to get what I want. I now know I want nothing to do with this. The only reason I will come anywhere near coercion is to stomp it out. And this, I fear, is my Achilles heel in this battle I fight within me. The rage that is left unattended in me is something I do not know what to do with.

"I've been stomping out these battles inside me for so long I don't know any other way, and I'm afraid it's no longer working. I was a sheep that strayed from your flock, Divine Creator. I went away from my faith, a faith that was fleeting and held no meaning. And in many ways, I'm glad I did. In my departure, I've come to think for myself. Dogma and doctrine no longer guide me. My mind and my heart guide me, and they have led me back here, to the center of myself where I have found you and the love you hold. I rest in peace knowing I am in you and you are in me. I trust you to lead my heart forward.

"I Am Yours forever in Christ. Your Sun, Michael."

Chapter 15 – Mystique and the Relational Space

The hours of laboring to construct the art studio left him both drained and rejuvenated. The reflection of creating a space, to allow for the creation of art never failed to inspire him. Yet the days labor left the residue of physical fatigue lingering in his cells.

"What in the piss is this cat doing to my tailbone," he said out loud as he lay with only underwear on, face down on his bed after having taken a shower. His new black cat, Mystique, a female from the litter of one of his landlord's cats now roamed his relational space. He got Mystique as a small kitten of 5 weeks when he first moved to Missouri. Now, several months later, the connection to his new soul traveler had been made. *Her flippin claws are sharp as shit... it's the most beautifully painful orgasm I've ever had... wait, is this weird that I'm orgasming from my cat massaging my tailbone...you know what, eff it, I don't care if it's weird, this shit is helping me open.*

This wasn't the first time Mystique had facilitated a deeper connective experience with him. The first was when she sauntered on to his chest one evening, as he lay resting after a particularly intense session of body integration. Mystique laid length wise on his chest, parallel with Michael's spine. Purring on all cylinders.

In Michael, an immediate recognition of love resonated with each melodic wave of her purr. He made a distinct decision to be okay with it. And with the decision came an escalation of energy.

An immense love enveloped Michael's body. It was a radiating joy that related to nothing in particular. Mystique responded by lightly pressing onto Michael's chest with her claws. That only served to heighten the experience.

Now, as Michael lay there, with Mystique once again doing her thing to his tailbone, he was more capable of being in a deep space of allowing. Being a neutral observer to the unfolding experience before him.

150

As he lay, the word *synergy* arose quietly in his mind. Deep in the center of his mind, he saw the word float across his imaginal landscape. A feeling of joy arose in his chest as he observed the word in his mind.

Slowly, the word descended as an image in his mind's eye, into a soft hum in his throat. Michael could hear a subtle buzz of insects outside his window. He moved the pitch of his hum in a harmony of resonance with the buzzing insects. As the harmony reached an equilibrium in his body, a bolt of electricity shot from the base of his skull down to his tailbone.

As you enter synergy in cognizance of your unity… a voice softly rose from his heart, working its way to the base of his skull, and out through his brow; to be projected as words on the screen of his mind's eye… *a movement of your paradigm will necessarily shift.*

Joy flushed through his heart as he lay there in a contemplative space. *There is no choice in your paradigm shifting or not. Your choice is to be willing to allow your consciousness to synergize…* visions of prosperity began cascading through the canvas of Michael's imagination… *into a cognizance of the primary root from which your existence stems from.* The vision coalesced into a point-of-view perspective, riding atop a dragon. Wings spread wide. Gliding through the air.

A surge of energy pulsed through Michael's spine, and in his heart. Below him, he could see the circuitry of energy that was his body, become one with the energy circuits of the dragon. Michael immediately knew that this was the ultimate message of Mystique.

The implicit energetic connection to all life can be harnessed into a synergy of expression. The word *tantra* arose in his space; followed by an immediate disgust of the recent articles he had been reading on Tantra. Articles that spoke of it only in the context of increasing sexual performance and pleasure. The disgust resonated as

151

a thought of beauty inherent to a sacred art that was distorted and slung as crack to unwitting souls.

Michael took a deep breath, acknowledging the disgust in him as a que to embrace the dignity of the deeper aspects of unity in himself. *This depth of unity is the unity of yoga as well,* he thought to himself. *All these arts have a much richer possibility available. It is our responsibility as conscious agents to bring what is within us, out.* Michael smiled as he recognized that thought and its similarity to a verse in the Gospel of Thomas. *I guess it does help to read sacred texts... hashtag KrishnaSaidThat... haha... and now I'm laughing out loud in my mind... hashtag KeepinMissouriWeird.*

Smiling to himself, he continued to lay there, face down as he had been for the last several minutes. Mystique continuing to resonate in chill-mode on his back. Paws over his tailbone. *Your destiny to rise from the disease of mediocrity is now yours to create. Where are you guiding the focus of your attention-point, young one?*

~ *I Am* ~

Facing Revelation

The Shadow World

Hiding its every thought,
Concealing its every direction,
Knowing only what is not,
Forgetting the One *Intention.*

Upon waking to the light
The shadows disperse from sight,
For inside the illumination
Is a heavenly exaltation.

Forward from the instant,
There is only Life.
Knowing only this instance,
Is living the only Life.

Miracles and miracles and miracles,
They beset the path of Life,
And then Life is the miracle,
For it is eternally Light.

A mind in shadows turns away,
A heart in shadows closes down,
And yet,
Here is this instant upon you,
For you to choose…
Will you turn away and close down,
Or smile, sing, laugh and play…

Come, let us turn toward light,
It shows us the way…

<u>Appendix A</u>

Dear Command Staff,

Please consider the following with the utmost un-biased view on the course of events that have led to the stand that I now take.

> When in the Course of human events, it becomes necessary for one people to dissolve the political bands which have connected them with another, and to assume among the powers of the earth, the separate and equal station to which the Laws of Nature and of Nature's God entitle them, a decent respect to the opinions of mankind requires that they should declare the causes which impel them to the separation.

> We hold these truths to be self-evident, that all men are created equal, that they are endowed by their Creator with certain unalienable Rights, that among these are Life, Liberty and the pursuit of Happiness. --That to secure these rights, Governments are instituted among Men, deriving their just powers from the consent of the governed, --That whenever any Form of Government becomes destructive of these ends, it is the Right of the People to alter or to abolish it when a long train of abuses and usurpations, pursuing invariably the same Object evinces a design to reduce them under absolute Despotism, it is their right, it is their duty, to throw off such Government.

On the day of writing this letter, I came into some information that appalls me and makes me question being part of an organization that lets the circumstances occur, of which this organization is under the direction of the Commander In Chief.

What follows is a discourse on why I believe it is necessary for me to take a stand and oppose my contract that obligates me into service. Not that it is a choice, but rather my duty to faithfully uphold the Constitution of these United States, an oath that I took when I joined that obligates me to do so.

From the excerpt above, out the Declaration of Independence, the document that formed the union for which the Constitution was made, explicitly states that whenever any Form of Government becomes destructive of these ends, it is the Right of the People to alter or to abolish it – it is their duty to throw off such Government. The Preamble to the Constitution states "We the people of the United States, in order to form a more perfect union, establish justice..."

It has come to my attention that the trespasses committed in the current war in Iraq, under the direction of the Bush administration has evinced that such justice is not important. Therefore it is my right, and duty, to uphold the fundamental principle of the constitution, which is to "establish justice".

Thus, according to Article 33 of the Geneva Conventions "No protected person may be punished for an offense he or she has not personally committed. Collective penalties and likewise all measures of intimidation or of terrorism are prohibited." This means that "collective punishments" are a war crime. The term "protected person" refers to civilian populations, or those that have laid down their arms. According to Wikipedia,

> By collective punishment, the drafters of the Geneva Conventions had in mind the reprisal killings of (World War I and World War II). In the First World War, (Germans) executed (Belgian) villagers in mass retribution for resistance activity. In World War II, (Nazis) carried out a form of collective punishment to suppress resistance. Entire villages or towns or districts were held responsible for any resistance activity that took place there. The conventions, to counter this, reiterated the principle of individual responsibility. The (International Committee of the Red CrossICRC) Commentary to the conventions states that parties to a conflict often would resort to intimidatory measures to terrorize the population in hopes of preventing hostile acts, but such practices strike at guilty and innocent alike. They are opposed to all principles based on humanity and justice.

Now consider the definition of a "War Crime" as put forth in the Nuremberg Principles. "War Crimes: Violations of the laws or customs of war which include, but are not limited to, murder, ill-treatment of the civilian population of or in occupied territory or wanton destruction of cities, towns, or villages"

Also put forth in the Nuremberg Principles are "Crimes against humanity: Murder, extermination, enslavement, deportation and other inhumane acts done against any civilian population"

You might be wondering exactly what I am referring to that exhibits such indiscretion towards life. A few days after Bush was re-elected back into office there was an attack on Fallujah, in which White Phosphorous was used to blanket the city. Also, it is well documented that MK 77, a substance eerily similar to napalm, was used, and may still be used throughout the war.

It is important to note that the US signed a resolution to not use napalm anymore. Yes, MK 77 is technically not napalm; however, it has the same effect. Although the use of MK 77 is an outright disregard for the resolution to not use napalm, it is still not a crime because MK 77 is technically not napalm.

What concerns me, and obliges me to retract myself from service is not the use of napalm or MK 77, although those two substance are completely inhumane as noted by the UNs protocol to not use incendiary devices on civilian populations of which the US did not ratify for some reason. The obligation comes from the "wanton" disregard for civilian life, more specifically, the children, and this is why I am obliged, not only as someone sworn to uphold the constitution but as a moral being as well.

On Dec. 23, 2002, the U.S., under the direction of President Bush, ratified a UN "Optional Protocol to the Convention on the Rights of the Child on the involvement of children in armed conflict" It was signed by the US on July 5, 2000 and entered into force on Jan. 23, 2003.

The conflict in Fallujah took place in Nov. 2004, in which the city was attacked for reasons beyond me. What is important is that it was a "collective punishment" on both civilians and "insurgents" alike. More specifically, the attack had a direct effect on children. According to the protocol, this can also be seen as "War Crime". The actual circumstances that bring about the appalling nature of this attack, and of the war is the fact that people were burned alive, and there was no differentiation between combatants, civilians, and children in particular.

The protocol entails,

> Condemning the targeting of children in situations of armed conflict and direct attacks on the objects protected under international law, including places that generally have a significant presence of children, such as schools and hospitals.

> Noting the adoption of the Rome Statue of the International Criminal Court, in particular, the inclusion therein as a war crime, of conscripting of enlisting children under the age of 15 years or using them to participate actively in hostilities in both international and non-international armed conflicts.

> Considering therefore that to strengthen further the implementation of rights recognized in the Convention on the Rights of the Child there is a need to increase the protection of children from involvement in armed conflict.

From the excerpt above, it is clear that any disregard for children in armed conflicts is illegal, and the disregard that was displayed in Fallujah is of that illegality. The actions were illegal because Fallujah was targeted, in which children lived, thus, the targeting of Fallujah was also "targeting of children in situations of armed conflict".

Up to this point, I have not been in support of the war, but I did not see any reason to outright oppose it. I have also shown interest in deploying, but at the time, I was not fully aware of the actual specifics of the situation in Iraq.

Not to mention the fact that children ARE being enlisted by the "insurgents", of which they are being involved in armed conflict. The enlistment is not being done by the U.S., but the actions that we have taken have resulted in children being involved.

Now that I am aware of the extent that the Bush administration is willing to go, I do not want any part of this inhumane treachery. It is my moral conviction, and firm knowledge that peace is an all prevalent force that can come about if each person dutifully puts forth effort to bring it about in the self.

Not only was the treatment of the civilian population in Fallujah against every fiber of my being, it goes against protocols that Bush himself has ratified.

Now, according to "command responsibility" even though Bush was not in Fallujah, he is still responsible for the treatment of the civilian population because he is the Commander in Chief, it was his idea that put the situation of Fallujah into existence.

Which brings me back to my original point,

When in the Course of human events, it becomes
necessary for one people to dissolve the political
bands which have connected them with another,
and to assume among the powers of the earth,
the separate and equal station to which the Laws
of Nature and of Nature's God entitle them, a
decent respect to the opinions of mankind
requires that they should declare the causes which
impel them to the separation.

That whenever any Form of Government
becomes destructive it is the Right of the People
to alter or to abolish it when a long train of
abuses and usurpations, pursuing invariably the
same Object evinces a design to reduce them
under absolute Despotism, it is their right, it is
their duty, to throw off such Government.

In no way do I suggest overthrowing the government, but it is
reasonable for me to assume my current stand on the situation
because as the first line of the Constitution of the United States
says "We the people of the United States, in order to form a
more perfect union, establish justice". According to resolutions
agreed to by the Geneva Conventions and Protocols enacted by
the UN, which Bush himself ratified, the "justice" that is
established by the Constitution, and the Geneva Convention,
and UN Protocols is being negated by the actions of the current
war. It is my responsibility and duty, not only as a citizen of
these United States, but as a sworn NCO (non-commissioned
officer) of the United States Army, to uphold the established
justice of the Constitution.

To uphold this "justice" I can no longer be a part of the organization that allows the treachery to continue, the organization being the Department of Defense.

In no way does my view reflect on your staff or anyone that I have been involved with thus far. Before now, I was obliged to continue my contract, and I did it to the best of my ability. However, I now find myself obligated to discontinue my service to a leader that disrespects the Constitution from which he garners his power, a Constitution that is the supreme law of the land. Not only that, the actions that have taken place can justifiably be considered a War Crime; a War Crime against the protocols that which the leader himself ratified.

Hypocrisy to this degree in the leadership of the most powerful nation on Earth is against every notion our forefathers had instituted in the Constitution. The situation in which I find myself is not of personal desires because personally, I would like to stay in and learn everything I can from the best leaders I have ever known. However, the situation is of principle, and it is of a principle that is of the highest esteem in human dignity. It is beyond any personal convictions, desires, or beliefs. It is of "self-evident truths" that speak to the nature of life that I must take this stand.

I hope that you take this with every bit of un-biased resolve and understand that I can no longer support a leader, an organization, or a war that is unjust. In no way does my attitude reflect on the soldiers that make-up the organization or the leaders that I have been directly involved with, my attitude goes directly to the top and surrounds the approved actions and reasons this war is taking place. Please consider that I do not intend to vilify anyone, or anything, but actions speak louder than words, and a picture is worth a thousand words. Both of which gives me plenty of reason to conclude that Bush is no longer suited to be the leader of the military or the United States.

Please know that I cannot stand idly by when innocent civilians, especially children, are being indiscriminately exterminated on the basis of location to insurgents. EVERY precaution must be taken to ensure the protection of the innocent, even though the innocent make take arms against you. In no way should children be considered targets in war, and if they are, something is SERIOUSLY wrong, and a different approach MUST BE TAKEN. I understand that there will be cases in which it is inevitable, however, a battle such as Fallujah is a War Crime, and those responsible are exactly that, responsible, and as such they are accountable for their actions and must answer to the consequences. This war is no longer a peace movement against terrorism when we become the terrorists. When civilians are indirectly targeted, it is an act of terrorism and we are no better than the "terrorists".

Not to mention, that we as soldiers adhere to values: Loyalty- Bear true faith and allegiance to the U.S. Constitution. Duty- Fulfill your obligations. Respect- Treat people as they should be treated. Selfless-Service, Put the welfare of the nation, the Army, and your subordinates before your own. Honor- Live up to all the Army Values. Integrity- Do what's right, legally and morally. Personal Courage- Face fear, danger or adversity.

According to these values, I am obligated that I take this stand. I cannot speak for anyone else, but this is the way the way I see the facts. Bear in mind that that this is not a personal quest because I would rather not do this, but I see it is a moral and legal obligation.

Thank you for your time, and consideration. Please know that this is nothing personal against anyone, but rather, a matter of universal principles that I take this stand, and the best thing that I have learned from your leadership, is that a leader must lead by example.

With Utmost Respect

Sgt. Michael J. Morris

__About This Book__

This book is written as a creative fiction based on certain perspectives of actual events. The characters in this story are based on real people. However, the depiction of the characters only represents the perspective of an artist telling a story and do not necessarily imply a factual disposition of a real person.

Each chapter acts a narrative summation of many situations. More than that, I as an author, have taken a great many creative licenses in the art story telling. The way the characters are depicted in this story is only my perspective creatively expressed.

Whether or not the way I depicted someone and its correlation to any degree of reality is irrelevant. I leave you to discern the nature of others based on your own experience and reflections.

I hope you enjoyed it. And I hope you have come to insight for your own life that you find to be useful.

Much Love & Many Blessings.

Other Titles by Michael Phoenix

Visit https://MichaelPhoenix.me for more.
- "Of the First Magnitude" series
  - o   iRise: An Algorhythm of Freedom
  - o   Quantum Engineering: Introspecting the Rabbit Hole
  - o   Algorhythmic Insight: Poetic Analysis of the Journey
- Body Integration & the One Minute Workout: Learning to Love the Body You're In

Of The First Magnitude

~I~

~Volume 1~
Facing Revelation
Emerge

~Volume 2~
iRise
An Algorhythm of Freedom

~Volume 3~
Quantum Engineering
Introspecting the Rabbit Hole

~Volume 4~
Algorhythmic Insight
Poetic Analysis of the Journey